Spindles and the Giant Eagle Rescue

Spindles
& the Giant Eagle Rescue

•BARRY CHANT•

Tyndale House Publishers, Inc.
Wheaton, Illinois

Other books in the Spindles series:
Spindles and the Mystery of the Missing Numbat

Library of Congress Catalog Card Number 90-71916
ISBN 0-8423-6214-2
Copyright © 1976 by Barry Chant
All rights reserved
Printed in the United States of America
99 98 97 96 95 94 93 92 91
9 8 7 6 5 4 3 2 1
Cover Illustration by © Ted Enik
Interior Illustrations by Lorraine Lewitzka

Contents

Characters

1 **Spindles**—Timothy Thornton, whose father and mother own the Dusty Range sheep station.

2 **Redgum**—A great eucalyptus tree, wise and strong.

3 **Hippie**—Spindles' educated emu friend.

4 **Tank**—A dinkum Aussie goanna.

5 **Roo**—A kind, motherly, gentle kangaroo.

6 **Joey**—Roo's joey.

7 **Bilby**—A spritely, rhyme-speaking desert bandicoot.

8 **Gloria**—Bilby's mate.

9 **Gleam**—A chattering, excitable, but helpful galah.

10 **Krag**—An awesome wedgetail eagle.

11 **Bigi** (pronounced bi-jee)—Krag's equally awesome mate.

12 **Koorook**—A mean, nasty crow.

13 **Lonely**—The station's quiet stockman.

14 **Sleepy**—Lonely's loyal dog.

15 **Kamulla**—An aboriginal station hand.

16 **Mr. & Mrs. Thornton**—Spindles' parents

17 **Uncle Charlie**—Spindles' eccentric uncle

I

Spindles and the Black Snake

Spindles crouched low behind a rock.

Slowly and carefully, he raised his head. Suddenly, he dropped down again. Cautiously, he peeped out from the side of the rock. Again, he quickly withdrew.

Next he darted across behind a tree. Panting, he paused as still as a shadow. Again, he slowly eased his head out so that he could see around the side of the tree.

Now, he carefully raised the stick he was holding to his shoulder. He pointed it towards a scraggly bush and squinted along the top of it.

"Pow!" he said. His shoulder jerked back, and he hid again.

He repeated this action a couple of times, and then nonchalantly wandered out and walked towards the bush. He looked down to the ground, kicked something and appeared to turn it over with a heave of his leg.

"He's finished," he muttered.

The stick now ceased to be a rifle. It became a sword, and he walked along chopping the heads off any innocent bushes or clumps of grass that happened to get in his way. In his mind's eye, he was a Mongol chief now, ruthlessly disposing of his enemies.

After a while, he found himself near the great Redgum tree. He settled down in his favourite spot and just sat for a while.

"We got a magazine at our place the other day," he said. "It had something in it about a man who didn't believe the Bible."

He knew that Redgum would be listening and so he went on talking. Anyone else who saw him would think he was talking to himself. But that didn't worry him at all.

"He reckoned that the Bible was too old-fashioned and simple and said that believing the Bible is like trying to fight tanks with a bow and arrow."

"Who's trying to fight me with a bow and arrow?" demanded a rough voice behind him.

"Oh, not you, Tank!" said Spindles to the goanna. "'Tanks'—you know, the things they use in war."

"Well, what about them?" asked Tank.

"I was just talking about a man who said that to live by the Bible today was like trying to fight tanks with a bow and arrow," Spindles explained.

It was then that Redgum spoke.

"It all depends on who your enemy is," he said. "For an old enemy, a simple, old weapon is sometimes the best."

A couple of days later, Spindles decided he would spend the day rambling around the Range. He left home early, with a packed lunch in a bag on his back.

"Don't forget to take a piece of wire with you!" his mother said as he walked out the door. "There could be some snakes about."

"No, Mum. I won't," he answered.

He saddled his pony, and rode off. Half way to the Range, he realised that the length of wire was still leaning against the fence near the homestead.

"Oh, well," he thought, "I probably won't need it, anyway. Besides, if I do see any snakes, I can always kill them with a stick."

Anyway, every time he had taken a length of fencing wire with him before, he had never needed it. It was always a nuisance. There were plenty of sticks lying around. A decent sized stick would kill any snake, he was sure.

Soon he was at the Range, and there were Hippie, Joey, Bilby and Gloria waiting for him. Bilby, as usual, was dancing around and singing to himself. Joey was also quite frisky. Hippie, who had a good sense of humour, was nevertheless a little more settled than the others.

Spindles left his pony to graze, and together the whole group set off up the creek ready for a day's picnic. Soon Bilby had them all singing one of his home-made songs:

"We're off to see some new gullies,
With rocks and scraggly mulga trees,
And yackas, scrub and spinifex
Which drops its prickles down my neck!"

It was not very musical. The high pitched voices of the bandicoots, the dull monotone of Spindles' tuneless song, Joey's soft childish tones, and the firm, strangely cultured voice of the emu, all made an unusual combination. But they were happy, and they sang the lines over and over again.

Redgum could still hear the echo of the voices long after they disappeared from sight.

They climbed the ridge above the head of the creek, and stopped for a while at the Opal Pool. Spindles drank from the cold, clear water, just as the animals did. It was here that Gleam joined them, and his raucous, chattering voice did little to improve their harmony!

They wandered along the top of the ridge for a while, and then made their way down a small gorge. The ground dropped away quite sharply and it was a steep climb. At first, the going was pretty rough. They clambered over small rocks, and through spinifex, dead branches, dry leaves and bushes as they penetrated further into the gorge.

Soon, however, they were at the head of the creek—although it was perfectly dry as usual—and following a small kangaroo track.

The scrub was fairly thick, and there were plenty of rocks, so it was not possible to see far ahead. And, of course, the path wound in and out among the scrub, sometimes following the sandy creek bed, and sometimes forcing its way through the bush.

Spindles found himself brushing leaves out of his eyes at times, or stooping to pass beneath a low hanging branch. Once, they found a large fallen tree trunk right across the gorge, and they had to get past it. Most of them had no trouble. Spindles and Roo easily clambered up and over. The two bandicoots found a way underneath. Gleam, of course, flew over. Hippie found it a little more difficult.

His long emu legs were excellent for running, but not so good for climbing— especially as he had no hands. Even his tiny wings were quite useless.

But he found a place where he could stretch one leg over the top, and then, by shifting his weight, he actually overbalanced to the other side.

Spindles was out in front now, and striding along, concentrating on avoiding the twigs that threatened his eyes, or the prickly spinifex that would scratch his legs.

So it was no wonder that he didn't see, at the side of the path, the grey scaly head with its beady eyes and flickering tongue, until he had nearly put his foot on it. Its body was hidden from view by a rotting log.

Spindles stopped, frozen, with one foot poised in mid-air. Joey bumped right into him, nearly causing him to overbalance!

"You might give some warning before you just stop like that!" he protested.

Spindles didn't answer. He just stood there, his eyes glued to the creature which lay before him.

Then Joey saw it, and so did Bilby and Gloria.

They all stopped in their tracks. Finally, Hippie who was bringing up the rear, stretched his long neck over Spindles' head to see what they were looking at.

The sinister grey head had not moved. The dark eyes stared unblinking. And the black tongue flickered again.

Suddenly from above, there came the sound of a chuckle. It clicked and rolled into a laugh. And then into shrieks of laughter. It was Gleam, sitting on a branch above them.

For a fraction of a second, Spindles took his eyes off the ground and looked up to see what Gleam was laughing at.

He couldn't see a thing.

He quickly shot his gaze back to the ground again. The mean-looking head was still there.

Then, Bilby started to giggle. And so did Gloria. And so did Joey. And Hippie.

Suddenly, the creature before him moved. It opened its mouth wide in a fierce hiss. Spindles could see a long black tongue and a bright pink mouth, with shining white teeth all around. The tongue flickered and there was another hiss.

And now Spindles started to laugh, too. He knew that sight and knew that it was not nearly as fierce as it looked. It was just an old sleepy lizard!

As it now moved out of the shadows, its legs could be plainly seen. It slowly wandered across the track, into the grass on the other side, hissing as it went.

Bilby broke into song. He jumped up and down as he sang, enjoying himself immensely:

"Spindles thought he saw a snake,
And trembled in his gizzard.
He should have been more wide awake,
'Twas just a sleepy lizard!"

The others tried to join in, and soon they were all chanting the song—all, that is, except Spindles. But he wasn't too upset. At first glance, they did look very similar, snakes and lizards, especially if you could only see their heads.

After four or five times through, they stopped that song, and continued walking.

Although they had all laughed, the incident with the lizard made them realise how easy it would be to step on a real snake. Especially for Spindles.

The animals were more naturally alert to the dangers of the bush, and less likely to be caught by them. But Spindles didn't have the same instinctive defences that they had. From now on, he was a little more watchful. Sometimes, it's a good thing to have a bit of a fright.

Bilby, too, realised how easy it would be for Spindles to accidentally tread on a snake. So he decided to help him. As he walked, he began to hum another little ditty:

> "Don't put
> Your foot
> Without
> A look!"

And at the end of each line, he deliberately and carefully put each foot down, as if marching to the tune. Soon they were all joining in, marching in line, with exaggerated steps, and, in the case of Spindles and Joey, their arms swinging. Gleam flew ahead like an army scout.

And so they continued down the gorge, a strange assortment of creatures, singing aloud as they went, over and over,

"Don't put
Your foot
Without
A look!
Don't put
Your foot
Without
A look!"

The ironic thing was, that the more they sang about taking care, the less care they actually took! They became so engrossed in the song, that in fact they began to put each foot without a look at all.

Spindles was striding along like a soldier, a piece of stick over his shoulder like a rifle, his head held high, and his feet stomping up and down like drumsticks, beating a measured time.

Even Hippie, who ought to have known better, was trying to join Spindles in his military style. His head, instead of moving backwards and forwards as it usually did when he walked, was being held erect—which meant that he could not see as clearly as usual—and his big feet were slapping down on the ground like fly-swats.

In view of all the noise they made, it is a wonder that there was anyone left in the whole of Dusty Range! You would think that every bird and beast would have fled for his life—or at least for peace.

But it was not so.

Ahead of them, there was a gap in the trees. The ground was sandy and smooth and deliciously warm in the morning sun. The high cliffs on either side sheltered the spot, and the gully winds that blew morning and night had somehow died away to enjoy a noon-day rest. And there, right where the path entered the clearing, looking for all the world like just another shadow from the overhanging branches of the surrounding trees, lay a large, black snake.

Out of breath from all the singing, and starting to feel hungry, the six friends had stopped their noise and were now trudging more quietly along.

Spindles saw the clearing and thought, "That would be a good place to stop for lunch."

He turned to suggest the idea to Hippie. Just as he did, he caught that black shadow in the corner of his eye. Something about it made him look again.

His heart nearly missed a beat. His whole body froze. Another two steps and he would have trodden right on to the shiny, black body of the snake. He could almost feel the squirming reptile beneath his feet, and then the red-hot jab of its fangs in his leg.

This time, everybody else stopped quiet and still, too.

No one moved.

No one spoke.

Spindles stood there, his gaze transfixed by the snake. Beads of sweat were standing out on his brow. Behind him, at his feet, were the two bandicoots. They, too, were motionless. Young Joey normally found it impossible to stand still for more than a few seconds. This time, you would have thought he was a grey rock, so unmoving was he. And Hippie, too, like an old grass tree, looked as if he had been growing there for fifty years. Gleam settled on a nearby gum branch, watching closely for every move.

The black snake did not stir. But its eyes were open and Spindles knew that they were fixed on him. He was so close, that if he moved, the snake might well move more quickly. And he could only go forward. With the others behind him, there was no way back. To go forward was to go closer to the snake.

Then, he remembered what his mother had said, "Don't forget to take a piece of wire with you!" If only he had it with him now. With a swift, lightning stroke, he could swing the wire down on to that deadly black creature before him, and its back would be broken in an instant. Then, it would be powerless and easy to kill.

But he had no wire.

All he did have was the stick that he carried over his shoulder as a gun.

When he had left home, he had told himself that a stick would do just as well as a piece of fencing wire. Now that he was faced with the reality of it, he wasn't so sure. But what else could he do?

Slowly, very slowly, he transferred the stick from his left hand to his right hand. The snake watched his every movement.

What happened next was so quick, that it was only afterwards that Spindles sorted it all out. For in about ten seconds several things occurred.

First, he grasped the stick firmly, tested his grip to be sure, and suddenly swung it hard on to the still form of the snake.

The point of the stick hit the ground and broke off. The rest of the stick didn't touch the

ground or the snake at all, but simply formed
an angle from Spindles' hand. A piece of wire
would have flattened out along the ground for
a metre or so, and then angled upwards. In
doing so, it would have fatally injured the
reptile. But Spindles did not have a piece of
wire. He only had a stick. And it was no good.

Spindles was still bending over from his
stroke with the stick, when the snake moved. It
darted towards him with its tongue flickering
and its fangs ready to bite.

He swung again, but the stick was a dry
one, a piece of gum, and it simply broke again,
this time into three pieces. The snake was
unharmed. Its head rose up to Spindles' knee
level. It drew back ready to strike. Spindles
was trying to recover from his second stroke.
His brain was telling his legs to run, but they
seemed to be stuck in the ground like fence
posts and would not obey.

He saw the ugly gleam in the snake's eye.
He saw that little black tongue. He saw the
sunlight glittering from the red and white belly
of the reptile as it held its head poised.

He knew that he could not escape.

So, too, did the others. They all moved
now. To clear the track behind Spindles, the
bandicoots dived sideways and Joey sprang up
on to a rock. Hippie moved forward, wanting to

do something to help, but not knowing what he could do. Gleam was already in flight, swooping down from his tree, although he, too, did not know how he could possibly help.

And then, there was a grey blur of movement. From out of the bush came a rocket, sleek and smooth, its cone shining with a strip of white and its tailfins stretched out behind.

Straight into the snake, it charged, grasping it behind the head.

The rocket was Tank.

The goanna's teeth gripped tight. The snake's body whipped around, its tail thrashing. Tank was thrown momentarily off balance by the combination of his own speed and the violence of the snake's reaction. But he did not let go.

The two creatures tumbled and whirled in the sand. It was a strangely silent affair. None of the spectators could say anything, transfixed as they were by the sudden drama. And the two struggling reptiles had no time for words. Only the grunts and hisses could be heard, with the noise of thumping and rolling and spraying of sand.

It was, in fact, all over fairly quickly. Tank never let go and his relentless, fatal grip gradually squeezed the life out of the snake. Its

movements became less vigorous, and gradually after a shudder or two, it became still. Tank stood there with the limp form of his enemy hanging from his mouth like an old bridle from a horse.

It was only then that he relaxed his grip, and the snake's body dropped with a soft thump to the ground, where it lay lifeless and unmoving, but still, in its own way, awesome.

Suddenly, they all spoke at once.

"Tank!"

"Where did you come from?"

"Boy! What a fight!"

"How did you get here?"

"You saved our lives!"

"Jolly good show, old chap!"

And, in spite of his shock and bewilderment at the sudden spate of events, Bilby managed four lines of verse on the spot to mark the occasion:

> "Who's the one we have to thank,
> For saving Spindles' life?
> None other than our good friend, Tank,
> Who rescued us from strife!"

It wasn't very good, but in the circumstances, they all thought it was excellent.

Spindles now recovered from his shock. Questions flowed out of him like machine gun fire. "Tank, where did you come from? How did you know where we were? When did you spot the snake? If you had been a minute later, I would have died! How did you do it? You really saved my life!"

"Where did I come from? 'Ow did I know you was 'ere?" repeated Tank. "With all the racket you was makin', I dunno 'ow anyone could *not* have known you was 'ere! I was just a bit further up the gorge, pokin' around when I 'eard your crazy song. So I decided to wander down to meet you.

"It so 'appened that I reached the clearin' at the same 'time as you lot. I saw the mess you was in, and knew that there was just one thing to do. I 'ad to get to that snake before you killed yourself.

"Fancy trying to kill a snake like that with an old dry stick. You oughtter know better!"

Spindles hung his head. He was too ashamed to admit that his mother had told him to carry a piece of wire, just in case.

They did stop there for lunch, but they were all very subdued. Spindles chewed his sandwiches without even knowing what was in them, and then he left half of them. The others found enough grass or roots to nibble to keep them going. When they returned home, they walked very carefully and quietly.

But they saw no more snakes.

A few days later, Spindles was sitting in his favourite position at the foot of the Redgum tree.

"Spindles," asked Redgum, "if you had taken a hand grenade or a rifle with you the other day, do you think you would have been any safer?"

Spindles thought about this for a moment. A grenade would have blown them *all* up. A rifle might have missed.

"No, I don't suppose I would, Redgum."

"And what about your stick? Was that any good?"

"No, Redgum. No good at all."

"What if you had taken some fencing wire?"

"That would have been alright."

"But isn't that what your dad used to carry when he was a boy? A bit simple and old-fashioned, isn't it?"

"What do you mean, Redgum?"

"Like the Bible?"

"Oh, I remember," Spindles said. "The man who said the Bible was too simple and old-fashioned. And you told me that it all depends on who your enemy is."

"That's right, Spindles. Sometimes, the old, tried and faithful weapons are the best ones. Modern ones are no use. And a substitute, like your stick, is worse still."

Spindles thought about that for a while. It seemed to make good sense. But Redgum had one more thing to say.

"Spindles," he continued. "Has God's enemy changed over the years?"

"No," replied Spindles. "He's still the same devil, I guess."

"Then neither has God's weapon," said Redgum.

That night, Spindles opened his Bible at the book of Ephesians. This is what he read:

And take the whole armour of God, that you may be able to withstand in the evil day. . . . Take the shield of faith with which you can quench all the flaming darts of the evil one, and take the sword of the Spirit, which is the word of God.
(Ephesians 6:13-17)

Somehow, it sounded very much like Spindles' mother saying, "Don't forget to take a piece of wire. . . ."

But this time, Spindles decided to take notice.

"Take the sword of the Spirit, which is the word of God," it said.

"Yes Lord, I really will," he answered.

2

Spindles and the Crystal Mountain

"Redgum," said Spindles. "You are always telling me to read the Bible."

Redgum stood silent and unmoving. There was no sign that he even heard what Spindles was saying. But Spindles was used to that and just kept on talking.

"But I find it so hard to understand. I mean, it's not really easy to follow, is it?"

There was still no answer. So Spindles continued. "Some parts are OK, I guess. But there's so much stuff about things that I don't know anything about." Spindles hesitated a moment. He wasn't sure whether he should say what he was thinking of saying next or not. Finally he decided he would.

"It's even boring in places," he ventured. "Once I tried to read part of the book of Levit—"

He stopped at that point for two reasons. First, he wasn't quite sure how to say

"Leviticus" anyway. Secondly, the strong, resonant voice of Redgum cut him off.

"Dig deep," said the voice. The words themselves were slow, firm and deep.

Spindles waited to see if Redgum would say any more. But he didn't really think he would. Sometimes when Redgum spoke, there was something about his words that told you that he had said all he intended to say and it was up to you to find out what he meant.

Hopefully, Spindles asked, "What do you mean by that, Redgum?" But, as he expected, there was no answer.

"Dip deep." What did that mean? What did it have to do with Bible reading? Spindles thought about it for a few moments, decided it was too much effort and promptly forgot all about it.

He stood to his feet and wandered away from the huge tree. The morning sun was bright in the azure sky, and it shimmered and sparkled along the edges of the gum leaves. A slight breeze cooled his skin as he walked and lifted his blond hair in tiny waves.

A few galahs and cockatoos could be heard in the treetops. Far overhead, hovering like black stars in the sky, were two eagles. Spindles shivered slightly, but knew that while they stayed up there, they were no danger to him.

Suddenly his aimless wandering was interrupted by the sound of a vehicle labouring across the plain. He ran back to the tree in time to see an old truck bouncing its way along the dirt road from the homestead. When it reached the creek, it pulled up.

"G'day young fellow," said the driver. "You must be Spindles."

Spindles didn't answer. He just stood there squinting up at the truck driver, who had stopped with the bright sun behind him.

"Just been up to the homestead and talkin' with yer dad," the man went on. "He said you might be down 'ere. I thought I'd like to meet you. 'Aven't seen you since you were a baby."

Spindles was very interested now, and interrupted, "How did you see me when I was a baby? Who are you?"

"I'm yer Uncle Charlie," he answered.

Uncle Charlie! The eccentric, wandering uncle who had no home. The strange man who loved the Outback so much that he spent all his time in remote areas. Whose lounge room was a clearing round a campfire. Whose bedroom was the back of his truck. Whose kitchen was a couple of billies on a campfire, or over the gas stove that he used when it was wet, jammed into a corner of the truck. Uncle Charlie! And here he was in person.

Spindles was delighted!

"'Op in, son!" said Uncle Charlie.

And Spindles did.

For the rest of the day, they drove, or sat, or walked together over the Dusty Range. And all day, Spindles listened fascinated to the stories his uncle told. Many of them, Spindles knew, were "tall stories"—stories that pass from person to person in the Outback until no one knows who started them or where they came from. But everyone feels, somehow, that they are his. For they belong to his country and are part of him.

With pleasure, Spindles heard Uncle Charlie tell of the summer that was so hot you could just crack eggs on to the hard, baked ground and they would fry in a moment.

Or of mosquitoes so big that wire netting would keep them out. (Then there were the really big ones—so strong that two of them held your arms down while the other one bit you!)

Or of the "hoop snake" that takes its tail in its mouth, forms itself into an upright circle and then rolls along like a child's hoop.

Or of the flock of cockatoos so thick that when it rained, not a drop got through to the ground.

But there was one story that really fascinated Spindles. And this one did seem to be true.

"'Ave you ever 'eard of the Crystal Mountain?" asked Uncle Charlie.

"The Crystal Mountain?" Spindles replied. "What's that?"

"Don't you know?" Uncle Charlie asked in surprise. "It's right 'ere in your own Dusty Range!"

Now Spindles was puzzled. "Well, I've never heard of it," he said.

"The Crystal Mountain is about six kilometres from 'ere," Uncle Charlie explained. "You can't drive in. You 'ave to walk, or ride yer pony or somethin'. That's why not many people know about it. But the 'ole thing is made of quartz. From top to bottom. All quartz. Of course, it's covered with grass and scrub and stuff, but that's only like skin on a rabbit. Once you get the skin off, the real thing is underneath. But you don't even 'ave to do that. You can just walk over it and pick up bits of quartz crystal. All different kinds, too."

Uncle Charlie paused for a moment, and then said, "'Ang on a minute. I reckon I've got a real beaut sample somewhere in me truck."

And with that, he began to rummage in the tool box under the front seat. And there, among the spanners and wrenches and screwdrivers and other tools, covered with dust and grime, he found a large piece of

quartz. He rubbed it on his shirt to "polish it up a bit" and showed it to Spindles.

It was about thirteen centimetres long and about two and a half centimetres thick. It was shaped like the pointed end of a garden stake, but six-sided. Its texture was like glass. You could almost see through it. In spite of the grease and scratches that it had gathered in Uncle Charlie's tool box, it was still a beautiful piece of stone.

"'Undreds of these lying 'round on Crystal Mountain," proclaimed Uncle Charlie. "You can just go an' pick 'em up."

That night Spindles lay in bed thinking about Uncle Charlie who had already gone on his way. ("No use me stayin' 'ere," he had said, "Couldn't sleep in one of your beds anyway. Too blinkin' soft. Rather use the back of me truck. Or the ground underneath—soft enough for me.") Spindles began to dream about Uncle Charlie's Crystal Mountain. He pictured it rising high in the sky, gleaming in the starlight, like some fairy palace. All over were glittering jewels. And he, Spindles, like an ancient prince, was gathering enough wealth for all the sweets, ice cream, money and servants he would ever need.

Next morning, he knew that his dream had been a bit far-fetched. But he also knew that he just *had* to find that mountain.

So, he set off on his pony, early, trying to remember Uncle Charlie's description, and determined to bring home a bag full of crystals.

He rode to the creek and up the creek bed. There he met Hippie and Roo and Tank and Joey. "How'd you fellers like to come exploring with me?" he called.

"Where?" asked Joey.

"Exploring?" asked Hippie. "What is there to explore? I know the whole place, old chap. Nothing left to discover, if you ask me."

So Spindles told them all about the Crystal Mountain.

"I know where that is," said Tank. "You should 'ave asked me in the first place. Anythin' about rocks and I'm yer man. Know all about 'em."

"Well," Spindles said to the goanna. "Lead on!"

So they climbed up the gorge, past the Opal Pool, down into a valley on the other side, over a few ridges, and along some creek beds until finally they approached the Mountain.

It would have seemed a strange procession to anyone else. In front, the darting, grey form of the goanna. Behind him, the emu, his long legs swinging and his head bobbing backwards and forwards with each step. Then the young kangaroo, bouncing along, constantly hopping aside from the track to inspect some insect or plant, and occasionally stopping, his head cocked on one side, to listen for he knew not what—but obeying the safety pattern built into him by his Creator.

And then, sitting easily on his pony, the young boy Spindles, his brightly coloured clothes in vivid contrast to the dull greys and browns of the animals, and his blond hair like a patch of tussock grass, caught by the breeze.

"Well, 'ere we are," growled Tank.

Spindles was surprised. Here was no shimmering castle. It hardly even looked like a mountain. Just another hill, rising untidily and roughly among the rest. He knew that his dream had been a bit unreal. But he hadn't expected the hill to be quite so drab.

"Are you sure?" he demanded of Tank. "I thought it was supposed to be all made of crystals and stuff."

"Oh that's all underneath," said Tank. "On the outside, it's just like any other hill. But get down off yer 'orse and poke around a bit. All these stones lyin' around 'ere—they're all quartz."

Spindles hopped down and began to fossick. He was looking for something like the one that Uncle Charlie had shown him. He couldn't find one anywhere.

Meanwhile Joey had found some tasty grass, Tank had stretched himself out on a sunny rock for a snooze and only Hippie was still with him. He dropped his long neck down to ground level, and peered at some stones lying there.

"I say, Spindles," he said. "What about those stones you're standing on? Somewhat different, aren't they? Seem to me to be rather good, actually."

Spindles stooped down and picked up a large stone. When he looked at it closely he was amazed. Instead of the one large crystal he had been looking for, he saw before him dozens of tiny crystals, heaped in a cluster like sugar in a bowl. They were bigger than sugar grains, of course. Each one was about three millimetres thick. And they were partly covered in red dirt—as if someone had tipped cocoa in the sugar! But he knew that, if he washed them, they would be very beautiful.

Now he began to look more closely. He fell to his knees, and scrambled among the stones, picking up almost every one he could reach.

He began to make other discoveries. He found one that looked like the piece of coral that his mother had sitting on the mantle piece at home. All over it were small rounded shapes, each with a tiny hole in it. He learned

later that this was called "pin-hole quartz."
Then he found another piece covered with tiny
crystals, two curved rows of them facing each
other like opposite sides of a large sea shell.
Another cluster of quartz was impregnated
with little black stones, as if someone had
deliberately placed them there to form a
pattern.

Then, with a shout, he found a single large
specimen. It wasn't as good as the bit that
Uncle Charlie had shown him, but it wasn't
bad. On one side it had been chipped, and so it
wasn't perfectly shaped; but it was about eight
centimetres long, and was obviously a genuine
crystal. Alongside of it, in the same sample,
were several smaller ones, some of them only
half formed.

Soon Spindles had a pile of stones about 30
centimetres high. "What are you going to do
with them, now you've found them, old chap?"
asked Hippie. "You'll never carry all of those
home."

But Spindles hardly listened. He was still
making discoveries.

In fact, he had climbed a little way up the
hill. In places he could see that there were
large outcrops of rock with pieces of quartz in
them. But most of it was indeed covered with
earth and scraggly grass and scrub.

About thirty metres up, he came across a big stone containing a very large crystal just poking out from the earth. He tried to lift it, but found it impossible. The more he struggled with it, the less likely it seemed to want to move.

So he found a large piece of stick—part of a fallen branch—and began to probe into the earth. He tried to force the stick under the rock and lever it up. But nothing seemed to give.

So he leaned on the stick with all his strength, trying to push it further into the ground.

Hippie was watching Spindles' efforts from down below with some amusement. Joey and Tank had lost interest altogether.

Suddenly, there was a shout from Spindles. They all looked in his direction, but could see nothing. Finally, they spotted him flat on his face. He slowly got to his knees, as the three animals ran up to see what had happened. When they reached him, in spite of themselves, they all laughed. For Spindles' face was covered in red dirt! An aborigine could not have done a better job with ochre.

"What are you doin' Spins?" laughed Tank. "Gettin' ready for a party?"

"No I'm not," said Spindles abruptly. "And don't laugh! I hurt myself!"

It appeared that as Spindles had pushed on the stick, it had suddenly given way and

completely disappeared into the hole he was trying to make. Taken by surprise, Spindles had fallen flat on his face. He was in fact a bit scratched, but it was nothing much and he soon got over it.

The next question was, what had happened to the stick? It had vanished.

They looked closely into the hole—which was, of course, only as big as the thickness of the stick—but couldn't see anything. Somehow, that stick had gone through the hole into the side of the Mountain.

"Where's it gone?" asked Spindles of no one in particular.

"Blowed if I know," said Tank.

"Search me," said Joey.

"Jolly interesting question," said Hippie.

"There must be a big hollow under there," suggested Spindles.

"Sounds reasonable," answered Hippie. "Must be something there. Sticks just don't disappear into thin air."

"Or thin mountains," suggested Joey.

"Ha, ha. Very funny," Hippie replied. "But you're probably right, Spins," he went on. "Obviously, the stick must have gone somewhere, I agree. There's probably a cave or something similar beneath. An interesting geological phenomenon."

"A what?" said Tank. "Speak English."

"Which, old chap, I was," Hippie responded. "If you don't know some basic scientific terms, then I can't be responsible for that. It's about time some people learned to speak the Queen's English. Now if—"

"I can speak all the English I need," Tank said firmly. "There's no need for you to start tellin' me—"

"Oh, cut it out you two," Spindles interrupted. "What I want to know is where my stick went."

"Well, you probably never will," put in Joey. "Let's go home now. I've had enough fossicking for one day."

It was in fact time to go, if they were to get home before dark, so they stopped their discussion, and set about the return journey. Spindles took one or two stones in his pockets, but had to leave most of them.

The next Saturday, Spindles was out at the creek again. This time he had a bag over his back, a small spade tied to his saddle, a torch, some food, a rope and a miner's pick.

"What are you going to do with all that stuff?" asked Joey in wonder.

"I'm off to the Crystal Mountain again," Spindles told him. "Want to come?"

"What for?" asked Joey.

"I'm going to try to find out what's under that rock. I want to see if there is a cave there."

"But that will take you ages," Joey argued. "You'll never do it."

"I agree, old chap," added Hippie who had just joined the conversation.

"Well, even if it takes all day, I am determined to keep digging until I find it."

"You might be sorry you said that," said Hippie knowingly.

"Well, I mean it," Spindles responded. "Who's coming with me?"

Hippie and Tank seemed to have little else to do, so they went with him. Joey decided to stay by the creek.

When they arrived, Spindles started digging with great enthusiasm. Stones, grass, dirt and dust flew wildly in all directions. Hippie and Tank kept well back. But after a while, when Spindles stopped to see how far he had got, he was surprised to find that all he had was a very small hole indeed.

"Is it safe to come out now?" called Tank, in a loud whisper. He was hiding behind a rock, and peeking out over the top in mock terror.

"Well, you weren't much help, anyway!" retorted Spindles, sharply.

And he resumed his digging. After a while he slowed down to a fairly steady pace and gradually the hole became larger, and so did the heap of dirt and stones behind him.

Hippie and Tank continued to make rude remarks like "If you were a grave digger, you'd be a dead loss" and "I'm glad you're not digging for water. We'd die of thirst waiting."

But he kept on.

In fact, with all that teasing, he had to! He couldn't stop now.

And slowly the hole grew larger.

By lunchtime, he was actually standing in it, up to his waist.

By mid-afternoon you could just see his white hair bobbing above the rim.

But then, he ran into trouble. Beneath him was solid rock. He couldn't go down any further. He struggled and heaved. He banged with his little pick trying to find a soft place. But there was no way down.

He couldn't understand it. That stick must have gone somewhere. It couldn't have gone straight through solid rock!

"Haven't you finished yet?" asked Tank.

"Oh mind your own business!" Spindles answered angrily. "Leave me alone!"

And he bit his lip to stop it quavering, and tried hard not to let tears well up in his eyes. It was so disappointing! So frustrating! So tedious! All that work and nothing to show for it. He brushed his sleeve across his eyes, stood up and climbed out of the hole. He stood there looking at it. There must be some answer! There had to be a way!

But it was time to go. Dispirited and dejected, Spindles climbed on to his pony, and headed for home. Hippie tried to make conversation, but it was no use. Tank decided it was safer to say nothing. Spindles just wanted to be left alone.

All the next week, Spindles felt angry. It would have been easy to give up altogether. After all, what did it matter where the silly stick had gone? But somehow it did matter—at least, to him. Now he had started, it seemed important to finish. He had to find out.

So next Saturday, Spindles again set out. And although they would rather have done other things, Tank and Hippie felt obliged to go with him, just out of loyalty.

When Spindles reached the hole, he examined it closely. There was certainly no way down, so there must be some other way. He tried to think back to the first time he had tried to force the stick into the ground. Then he remembered! He had been facing almost straight into the side of the hill. He had not been pointing down at all. Maybe if he tried to dig inwards, he might get somewhere!

He poked around with his spade and pick. There, right in front of him, between two large rocks, was a patch of dirt, soft enough to dig. He began to work on it. The top stone began to shift. He wedged his spade under it, and rocked it up and down. Suddenly, and for the second time, the unexpected happened.

Instead of moving upwards and out, the stone moved downwards and in! It simply caved in before his eyes. He nearly lost his spade in the process. Again, he himself fell to the ground, but this time without burying his face in the earth.

Before him was a dark, gaping hole, about the size of a basketball. By this time, Tank and Hippie were both looking down into the hole to see what was happening. Hippie's long neck reached down over Spindles' shoulder. "Fascinating, what?" he said.

Tank actually scampered down into the hole and poked his head under Spindles, peering into the darkness. "Stone the crows," he said. "There was somethin' there after all."

Feverishly, Spindles pulled at the earth and rock, throwing it between his legs and out behind him. Once again, Tank stood well aside. The hole grew quickly larger. Some of the earth fell into it, but he didn't worry about that.

Before long, he saw a kind of tunnel before him. He ran back to his pony, grabbed his torch and slowly crawled in. It was not really very big, but it was big enough for him. Dust and dirt fell into his hair and eyes. He scraped his knees on sharp stones as he crawled. Tank was close behind him, quite at home. But Hippie, of course, stayed outside.

The hole was very dark. Indeed, the further they ventured, the blacker it became. It was intense. But Spindles' torch was powerful. Its strong beam was like a tunnel of light within the tunnel of darkness.

He came to a slightly larger area and looked back. Already, the entrance was just a small white spot in a black world.

Then he started to crawl forward again. Suddenly the ground disappeared before him. In fact, he nearly tumbled forwards into the blackness.

With a shock, he put his hand out in front of him and felt nothing! He realised that he had come to the end of the tunnel, and that it had opened up into a large area—how large he did not know. Certainly it dropped away steeply beneath him.

A pebble or two fell from the edge while he was kneeling there. It was several seconds before he heard the noise of bouncing and clanging far below him.

I'm glad that wasn't me, he thought.

Then he began to shine his powerful torch around. As he shone it upwards, he was suddenly dazzled by ten thousand sparkling lights.

The roof of the cave was just above the level of the tunnel. And all over the roof, hanging in clusters like ripe fruit, were myriad crystals of quartz. Each of the varied faces of the quartz reflected back a tiny portion of the torch light.

Together the reflections were like a dozen Milky Ways on a clear night. It was a jeweller's shop. A grand hall of chandeliers. A cluster of diamond rings. All the glow worms in the world lined up together. A starry sky without the sky—just the stars. It was magnificent.

On other, later occasions, Spindles saw the cave lit up by several strong torches at once. Then it was really beautiful. But somehow, that first glimpse, by the light of a single torch stayed in his memory and filled him with wonder.

Spindles sat there a long time. Even rough and ready Tank was spellbound. Used to hiding between rocks and under trees, the goanna was accustomed to dark places. But he had never seen anything like this. A whole cave of crystals!

It was a long time before Spindles went home. When he did, his first wonder was lost in the excitement of discovery. And he could hardly wait to tell his parents about it.

"Well, exactly how did you find it?" his father asked, at the dinner table.

"I just kept digging," Spindles replied. "But I had to dig pretty deep. It took a long time."

"You know, Timothy," his father went on, "if this is as good as you say it is, this discovery could even make you famous. I'll look at it myself tomorrow. Then perhaps I'll let the Mines Department know. They're almost certain to send someone out. A cave full of crystals must be really rare.

But Spindles was not listening. Something he himself said had jolted his memory. "Dig . . . deep." Where had he heard those words before? "Dig deep." Who said it? Redgum? Yes, Redgum! He was the one.

In his room that night, Spindles began to think about it. It was a long time since he had read his Bible. "Too dull. Too boring," he had said. And Redgum had said, "Dig deep."

He reached for his Bible and it fell open at Colossians, chapter two.

This was a book that normally he would never have looked at. (Who would read a book with a name like that anyway?) But what he read now was: "Christ, in whom are hid all the treasures of wisdom and knowledge."

Treasures of wisdom and knowledge in Christ? It was a new thought. Perhaps these were like the treasures in the Crystal Mountain. You had to dig deep for them!

Spindles remembered how hard he had worked to find that cave. It had only started because he wanted to know what happened to his stick! If he could work so hard to find a stick, what about treasures that really mattered?

The next time he was at the Range, he sat down in his usual spot under the great Redgum tree.

"Redgum," he said. "Redgum, do you remember how you told me to dip deep if I wanted to understand the Bible? Well, I think I know what you meant now.

"In fact, I've found two treasures. A marvellous cave. And some marvellous truths in the Bible.

"I even read the Bible for half an hour straight the other night. And you were right. When I kept digging, I found lots of wonderful things!"

"Would you have found your cave if you had given up after being stopped by the rock in the bottom of the hole?" asked the Tree.

It didn't occur to Spindles to ask how Redgum knew all about his digging. Redgum seemed to know all kinds of things.

"No, of course I wouldn't," Spindles answered.

"So you had to keep on digging right up to the end?"

"Yes, Redgum."

"You know what I'm getting at now, Spindles?"

"Yes," said Spindles, "I know."

And he did too.

3

Spindles and the Open-Cut Mine

"I'm sick of being told what to do all the time," complained Spindles. "Do this, do that, do the other thing! Why can't I just do what I want to do?"

Spindles was sitting in his favourite spot under the Redgum tree. And he was fed up.

It seemed that his life was not his own. Every day his mother had tasks for him to do. Then his father always had something extra. Then there was his schoolwork. And when he read his Bible, it seemed to be full of instructions too.

"Do not steal . . . Do not tell lies . . . Do not judge . . . Do not envy . . . Do not hate . . . Obey your parents . . . Love your neighbour . . . Pray constantly . . . Stand firm . . . Resist the devil . . . Overcome evil . . . ." There was no end of them.

"Why is everyone always telling me what to do?" Spindles demanded again.

"Because they love you," said Redgum.

Redgum's voice startled Spindles and he sat up with a shock. He had almost forgotten the great tree was even there, he was feeling so sorry for himself.

"Eh?" he said, "What did you say?"

But there was no answer. There was no need of one, really, for Redgum knew very well that Spindles had heard exactly what he had said. Like most boys, Spindles usually said "Eh" out of habit rather than need. It was a useful practice that often gave him time to think of a suitable answer.

"Because they love you."

Spindles thought about it for a while, but couldn't see that it made much sense.

"If they loved me," he argued to himself, "they wouldn't make life so miserable for me. They'd let me do what I want to do for a change, instead of making me do what *they* want to do. I can't see much love in that!"

He got to his feet and wandered along the creek bed. He saw a pebble about the size of a cricket ball. He lined it up, carefully calculating the number of steps he would need, ran toward it, and kicked it hard.

The next moment he was jumping around on one foot, holding the other in his hands, moaning and groaning in agony. The stone remained unmoved, joined as it was, to a large slab or rock that lay beneath the pebbles, out of sight.

It didn't make Spindles any happier!

Even the stones hated him!

He limped his way further along the creek bed, muttering to himself.

"I say old chap, had an accident, what?"

Spindles looked to his right, and there, standing quietly among some mulga trees was his emu friend, Hippie. Until he moved, you would have thought he was part of the trees himself, with his greyish-brown feathers hanging like the long, thin leaves of the mulga, and his straight legs and neck for all the world like branches of the trees.

"Oh, mind your own business!" answered Spindles.

"Well, that's a nice friendly way to greet a fellow, I must say," retorted Hippie. "Your politeness overwhelms me, sir."

Spindles was about to say, "Don't be sarcastic!" or something similar, when he looked at Hippie, and saw the twinkle in his eye, and the way in which he was trying to look very dignified and offended, and he couldn't help but laugh.

"Oh, I'm sorry, Hippie," he apologised. "I nearly broke my foot a while ago, that's all."

Hippie had in fact seen what had happened

and decided it was better not to ask any further questions. He changed the subject completely.

"Did you know that the old feldspar mine is full of water again?" he asked Spindles.

"Is it?" Spindles answered.

"Absolutely," said Hippie. "Never seen so much water in it before. Must be thirty metres deep, give or take a few."

"Hippie!" said Spindles slowly.

"Well, twenty, perhaps."

"Hippie," said Spindles again.

"Fifteen?" suggested the emu.

Spindles was not really much good at estimating distances or heights himself, but he knew that Hippie's figures normally had to be divided by half at least.

"Well, let's go and see it!" cried Spindles.

And he sped away to his pony. Half-way there, he remembered his "nearly broken" foot and tried to limp a bit. Then he decided it wasn't worth it and kept running normally. Hippie chuckled to himself and nearby the Redgum tree smiled knowingly.

With Hippie loping along next to him, Spindles rode up the creek bed, slowing down to a careful walk as they neared the top of the gorge.

They picked their way along the ridge top,

then across a saddle and into a low, spreading pound about a kilometre wide. They crossed the pound and finally rounded some low hills to the north east. And there, in the foot hills, was the feldspar mine.

"Hey, you were right!" exclaimed Spindles. "It is full of water."

"Naturally," answered Hippie, modestly, lowering his eyes.

"Well, that hole is *mine*," Spindles added pointedly.

"Oh," Hippie groaned. "That must have required *deep* thought."

"It was very *down to earth* anyway," retorted Spindles.

"Sounds like an *open and cut* case to me," replied Hippie.

"That was a bit weak," Spindles answered.

"Well, it is an open-cut mine," Hippie went on.

"You don't have to explain it to me, Hippie," protested Spindles. "I can see that for myself. Look—you can almost imagine a huge hand holding a garden trowel, coming down out of the sky and digging a great path right through that hill!"

It did look something like that. If you can picture in your mind a hill with the middle cut right out of it—like a slice out of a steamed

pudding—and the cutting going right down
deep into the earth, then you can see what
Spindles and Hippie saw.

Large earth-moving equipment had cut a
swathe right into the hill. Three sides were
perpendicular. The fourth was sloping—the
side where the machines had entered. The
whole thing was now filled with water—dirty,
brown water like liquid mud. It lapped the
edge on the sloping side. The other three sides
rose straight out of the water, steep and high
and dangerous. Even on the shallow side, the
earth had been eaten away, and it was
perilously boggy and treacherous.

Spindles and Hippie moved down from
their vantage point and approached the near
side of the mine.

"What do they use feldspar for, anyway?"
asked Spindles.

"Jolly interesting question, that," answered
Hippie.

"Well, what's the answer?"

"Very simple, really," Hippie went on.
"Feldspar is a white, crumbly sort of rock. It
has mineral value, you know. So they use
bulldozers to excavate it and transport it away
for processing. Fascinating business really."

"You don't say," said Spindles. "Thanks for
the helpful information." Then he continued,

"Anyone can see it's a white crumbly rock. Look, there's still some of it there in the walls of the mine. And of course it has mineral value. Otherwise they wouldn't mine it. But what do they use it for?"

Hippie, of course, had no idea. Had he lived in the city and been familiar with modern kitchens, he might have known. For feldspar is one of the ingredients in some household cleaners which makes them clean "whiter than white." But Hippie didn't know about things like that.

"Well, to tell you the truth old chap," Hippie admitted. "I really don't know."

"That makes two of us," answered Spindles. "Hey look! There's a sign over there."

He pointed toward the edge of the mine. There stood a wooden notice. It had originally been a miner's claim, giving the license number and name of the owner. But over the top of the faded figures, in rough, thick letters, someone had painted:

DANGER—KEEP CLEAR—SOFT EDGES

"Must be dangerous," muttered Hippie, half to himself.

"S'pose it is," answered Spindles.

They stopped where they were for a few minutes, just looking over the mine.

"I wish I could see right down into it," Spindles said. "Then we could see how deep the water really is."

"I can see well enough from here, really," answered Hippie, his skinny neck reaching up high.

"That's all right for you, Hippie," Spindles continued. "But I can't."

This wasn't exactly true, for Spindles was sitting on his pony, and in fact could see just as well as Hippie. He seemed to realise this himself, for he jumped down quickly, as if to prove his point.

He began to creep closer.

"I say, Spins," Hippie said. "You can see what the sign says, can't you? Better stay back here."

"I'm not very heavy," argued Spindles. "That sign probably applies to grown-ups. I'll be all right."

"I don't care who it refers to," Hippie answered, "It's not worth the risk, really. I mean to say, old chap, if you fall in you'll be in a hole, rather."

"Ha, ha, ha," replied Spindles sarcastically. "Very funny."

"Look, Spins, I mean it. That sign isn't there for nothing."

"I'll be OK, Hippie," replied Spindles. "Stop worrying."

And he kept on walking slowly toward the edge. When he was almost there, he dropped to his knees and crawled the rest of the way.

Hippie and Spindles' pony stood well back.

Spindles was now right at the edge. He dropped to his stomach, lying full length on the ground. He slid forward so that his head poked over the edge. Actually, the ground seemed rather hard and the edge quite firm.

He looked down beneath him. The water level must have been at least twenty metres down. There was no way of knowing how deep it was. So much of the red earth from the cliffs around had fallen into it, and so much of the mud from the bottom seemed to have been stirred into it, that it was a thick, muddy brown. You couldn't see more than a centimetre below the surface.

He turned around to look at Hippie, putting more weight on to his left hand as he did so. He was just about to say, "Look, it's quite safe . . ." when the edge under his hand gave way and he fell flat to the ground, his left arm dangling over the edge. A piece of earth the size of a football crashed and splashed down into the murky water.

For a moment, Spindles' heart stopped beating and he caught his breath. He rested both hands on the edge again, and this time tested it with his weight before he turned around. The ground seemed firm enough.

"I told you it wasn't safe!" Hippie called out.

"It's all right," answered Spindles. "There was just one loose piece, that's all. You ought to look down over here, Hippie. It's really spectacular."

He turned around to look down into the water again, when to his dismay, something else happened. This time, the hat that he was wearing tumbled quietly off his head and drifted gently down to the water. Like a small boat it floated there, as if moored just off shore.

Now, normally this wouldn't have been a great loss. But this was a new hat, which his mother had just bought for him. She had insisted on his wearing it—in spite of his objections—because she thought it might stop his nose being so badly sunburned.

"Now, I'm in trouble," thought Spindles. "Mum will be furious if I lose my new hat! What can I do?"

"You'd better come back," Hippie called again. It's not worth the risk."

"But I can't," answered Spindles. "I've just lost my hat."

"Too bad!"

"But I can't go home without it! Mum will murder me!"

"Too bad," said Hippie again.

"It's all right for you. You don't have to face Mum!"

"I'd rather face her without a hat than not to face her at all!"

"You don't know my mum!"

"Yes I do. And I'd still rather face her without a hat than not at all."

Hippie, of course, had never actually "met" Spindles' mum, but he knew that she was a good mother and he knew that he was right.

Spindles, however, could not be convinced.

"I know what I'll do!" he suddenly shouted excitedly. "I'll climb down and get it."

"You'll what?" demanded Hippie, astonished.

"Climb down and get it! I can see a kind of path leading down just over here a bit. I reckon I can do it."

"You're crazy! There can't be a path there, old chap."

"Well," Spindles said doubtfully, "Not exactly a path—but I think there are enough places to hold on to be able to climb down."

And he began to climb over the edge.

"Spindles!" called Hippie. He was really worried now. "Spindles! Come back! You'll drown or something! Don't be idiotic!"

For a moment Spindles hesitated. He

realised that there was a sense of urgency in Hippie's voice. And, deep down, he knew that Hippie was right. Perhaps he should forget the hat. His mum would be cross, but she would probably understand.

Then, suddenly, he thought, *Now Hippie's trying to tell me what to do. Everyone's always pushing me around. Just for once I'm going to do what I want to do. I'm sick of doing what everyone else says!*

So he began to climb down.

Actually, it was not so difficult as it might have seemed from where Hippie stood. The cutting was pretty rough and there were plenty of hand and footholds. And in spite of the notice, the earth was fairly hard. For although the mine was full of water, it had been like it for some time and there hadn't been much rain.

Once or twice, bits of earth crumbled beneath him, but he was careful, and tested each ledge or outcrop before applying any weight to it.

Spindles was, in fact, a fairly good climber. He remembered how he had been stuck on a cliff once before and he made sure that he didn't over-reach himself this time.

Before long, he was down at the water's edge. There was a small ledge there just big

enough for him to stand on. It was partly
earth, partly rock, but it seemed solid enough.

His hat floated just out of reach.

He looked around and saw a bit of a bush
growing in the side of the cliff, and with some
pulling and pushing, he was able to dislodge it.
He broke off a stick about 60 centimetres long,
and reached out over the water.

Carefully he poked the end of the stick into
the hat and began to draw it in toward him.
The stick slipped and the hat started to sink.
He thrust the point of the stick under the hat
and kept it afloat. He gingerly pulled it in closer.
Then with one hand he held the stick and with
the other he carefully reached out for the hat.

He could just reach it.

With two fingers he picked it out of the
water and slowly straightened up. He dropped
the stick, and with both hands squeezed the
water out of the hat.

"I got it!" he shouted to Hippie.

There was no answer.

"I got it, Hippie!" he shouted louder.

There was still no answer.

His voice seemed to lose itself in the great
open mine. The breeze that blew across the
top flung it back to the water level. It seemed
that his voice was, like himself, cut off from the
rest of the world.

Hippie was still up there, of course. But he didn't know what to do. If he came close to the edge, he might fall in himself and then they would both be lost. If he stayed back and Spindles fell in, what could he do?

Hippie was really worried.

Why didn't Spindles call?

What was happening down there?

Spindles began to climb back up again. He needed both hands, of course, so he thrust the wet and dirty hat on his head. It was fairly hot down there out of the wind, anyway, so it didn't matter.

He could see where he had climbed down all right and he began to follow the same path up. At first the going was very easy. In fact, the whole climb was really not very difficult, although it was steep.

When he was about a third of the way up, he paused for a rest and called out again.

"Hippie! Hip-pie! I'm on the way up again! I've got my hat!"

There was again, no answer.

He climbed further. When he was about half-way, he stopped again and called.

"Hip-pie! I'm on the way up!"

This time Hippie did hear him. It was just a faint call that struggled up and over the edge before fading exhausted to the ground.

Hippie called back: "Jolly good show! Keep coming!"

But this time it was Spindles who heard nothing, for Hippie's voice was not strong enough to reach him.

Hippie looked at the sign: "DANGER," it said. "KEEP CLEAR—SOFT EDGES." Perhaps the edges weren't so soft after all. Maybe it was only after rain that there was any worry. Probably he was being concerned over nothing.

He began to relax. Suddenly he heard Spindles' voice again. "Hippie!" it called. But this time there was a sense of urgency about it. It was not reassuring like the cry before. It was desperate, fearful, terror-filled.

It was followed by a scream that faded away.

And then nothing.

Or was there the sound of splashing water?

Hippie now made up his mind. Even if there was a risk of his falling into the water, too, he had to know what had happened. His heart told him to run; his head told him to walk softly.

Tentatively, painstakingly, he approached the side of the mine. He reached the edge without difficulty, stopping half a metre back. He stretched his long neck forward until he could see over. Down below him, a long way down, he saw the small form of a boy struggling and splashing in the water. It disappeared and then emerged again thrashing and straining to keep above the surface.

"Come on old fellow," Hippie heard himself saying. "You can do it."

The small body disappeared and emerged again. This time it stayed a little longer on the surface, before going down for the third time.

Finally, Spindles reappeared. Hippie felt so helpless. He longed to do something. But what could he do from up there? Below him was a life and death struggle—and all he could do was watch, and pray.

"Please, God, help him!" he pleaded.

Spindles didn't know which way was up or down. The brown, muddy water was so dark that he couldn't even see his own body.

He tumbled and turned, until his head emerged into brilliant light and sharp fresh air. He gulped thirstily for air, but too late, and found his mouth filled with dirty water!

He spluttered and spat and struggled for the surface again.

This time, he managed to hold his head up a few seconds longer. He moved his hands and feet frantically, in a desperate effort to keep himself afloat.

But again, he bobbed under the surface,

and again the dirty water flowed into his nostrils and filled his open mouth.

This time however, just before he submerged, he caught a fleeting glimpse of the wall of the mine. Growing in it, right at the water level, was a small bush. Perhaps he could grab it, and hold on!

He forced his head above the water level again. He spat and sniffed, drew in a life-giving gulp of fresh, clean air and tried to splash his way to the bush. It was only a couple of metres, but it seemed much more. In that short distance, he sank twice and reappeared twice, swallowing more water each time.

But then, with a desperate lunge he flung his right hand out toward the bush. He felt its tiny, rough twigs between his fingers, as he tried anxiously to grasp hold of it. But his wet hand slipped, and he went down again.

When he came up however, he was directly under the overhanging branch. It was small—only half a metre long—and not very thick, but when he grabbed it with both hands, he felt it hold. He hung there for a few grateful seconds, heaving and panting, filling his lungs with refreshing, cool, cleansing air. After a while, the gulping subsided and he began to breath more normally.

Now he looked around to see where he was.

To his right was the small ledge he had stood on to fish out his hat. Perhaps ne could reach it. He let go with one hand and trusting his weight to the other, he stretched out for the ledge. He tried to find a footing for his feet, but the wall of the mine was so soft and slippery that it was hopeless trying to gain any support from there.

With his right hand, he managed to take hold of the ledge. He burrowed his fingers into it, to gain a firmer hold.

Without warning, a lump of mud broke off in his hand, and he fell back under the water! Fortunately, he had not let go of the bush with his left hand, and he was able to pull himself up fairly quickly. But again it was a time of spluttering, sneezing and wheezing for a few seconds.

He reached again for the ledge, but now that part of it had broken away, he could not even touch it without letting go of the branch. And this he was afraid to do. It seemed to be his only safety now.

He looked up to the top of the mine. He saw nothing.

Then he heard a distant, faint voice. "I say, old chap, are you all right?" He looked up again.

"Where are you, Hippie?" he called, breaking into another bout of coughing as he did so.

"Right here!" came the answer. "Can't you see me?"

Spindles looked, squinting his eyes as he did so.

The bright blue of the sky almost hurt him as he peered upwards. Then he saw Hippie's tiny head, a mere dark speck against the brown, earth wall of the mine.

Again Hippie called, "Are you all right?"

"I—I th-think so," he answered.

"Can you get out?"

"N-no. I d-don't think I c-can," replied Spindles. "Help me, Hippie! D-do something."

"Yes, indeed. Indeed I will," said Hippie. "Can you hold on for a while, Spins?"

Spindles tested the bush. He yanked at it. It seemed to be firmly rooted. Again he tried to find a place for his feet. The water was very deep, of course, but he found that if he burrowed his feet into the wall, it was soft enough for him now to make a small step to help him take the weight of his body.

"I—I th-think so," Spindles said again.

"I'll see what I can do. Hang on, old man," cried Hippie, in his creaky voice.

Hippie's small head disappeared.

"Wh-what am I g-going to d-do?" Spindles asked himself.

Suddenly he became aware of the fact that

he was very cold. He realised now why he had been stuttering. He remembered having read somewhere of people dying of cold. What if it happened to him?

He became very frightened.

And he wondered how long he would be able to hold on to the branch before he became so weary that he would fall down into the murky water—perhaps for the last time.

He tried not to think of it.

Above the mine, Hippie thought desperately, wondering what to do. Somehow, he had to get a message back to Spindles' home. How could he do it?

Nearby, Spindles' pony was standing quietly grazing.

Perhaps he could get the pony home?

Slowly he approached the animal and with his beak picked up the rein that was dangling and trailing on the ground. He lifted it quietly, and holding his head high, stretched it out till he could feel tension between his beak and the pony's mouth.

If the horse wanted to, he could jerk the rein from Hippie's beak with one flick of his head. Hippie began to step forward. He felt the pony resist for a moment or two. What would he do?

Then Hippie felt the pressure ease, as the

pony also stepped forward. Hippie took another step. So did Spindles' horse. A third step. A fourth. And so they moved on together.

It was a strange sight, the pony meekly following the emu's leading.

For a few hundred metres they walked on together like that. But Hippie knew the time was short. He had to get help quickly. What if he started to run? Would the pony follow? Or would he resist, and thus prevent him from getting help at all?

It was a risk, but a risk that Hippie had to take.

He quickened his pace, finally breaking into a loping swaying canter. The pony also began to run. Hippie found it hard to stop his head swaying backwards and forwards as it usually did when he ran. But he managed to do so.

Over the foothills they went. Then across the pound. As they approached the saddle, their pace had to slow down. Then, they mounted the ridge and had to walk again, more carefully now for it was fairly steep, and they could take no risks. Finally they were picking their way down the creek bed toward Redgum.

Here, Joey bounced up, demanding, "Hippie! What are you doing? Where's Spindles? What's happened?"

And Gleam flew overhead, screeching out similar questions.

Hippie, his beak full of bridle, could only answer, "Shpindhsh hash fasn insha mine."

"Eh?" asked Joey.

"What did you say?" asked Gleam.

But Hippie had no time to explain. They were now on flat ground and he again broke into a run. The pony followed. Across the plain to the homestead they ran, like two beetles joined together, the empty stirrups bouncing and flashing in the sunlight at the pony's side.

They reached sight of the homestead, and Hippie at last had to drop the bridle and leave the pony to go on alone. The animal needed no further encouragement. Already sensing the smell of fodder and a pleasant rest in the shady yard, he trotted toward the stable.

Here, Butch noticed the riderless horse.

Thinking that Spindles had just dismounted and left the pony, the station hand began to call him, angrily. "Spindles!" he shouted. Didn't the boy know that a good stockman always put his horse first?

He called again, but there was no answer.

He walked out into the homestead grounds. Spindles was no where to be seen. Then he looked more closely at the pony. The saddle was dusty as though no one had been on it for a while.

Butch became alarmed now, and ran to the house.

It was not long before Spindles' parents and Butch and Lonely and the cook were all gathered in the yard. Obviously something had happened. No one had seen Spindles. The pony had come home without him.

A search was organised and within minutes, Mr. Thornton was driving down the track toward the creek in his four-wheel drive vehicle. Butch was racing off to the south. Lonely was on his motorbike, with Sleepy, his dog, on the back. He rode out the gate, thinking as he went. Spindles would not have gone west or north. It was too dry and barren in those directions. He never went there.

Mr. Thornton was checking the creek area. Butch had the south covered. What about the back of the Range? Perhaps he was there, around to the north-east.

So he slipped into a higher gear and rode as fast as he could in that direction. The little bike bounced and slithered over the rough country. Sleepy stood in the back, seemingly unconcerned, keeping his balance in expert fashion.

Around the ranges they went, along the back of the ridge which Spindles had crossed on his way to the mine, and toward the very same low hills where Spindles was.

Lonely called as he rode. "Spindles! Spin-dles!"

But there was no answer.

He stopped at the foot of Bilby's hill. There was no sign of him there. He continued to ride on.

Meanwhile, Spindles was growing ever more weary and cold. His whole body was shaking and shuddering. He had lost the feeling in his feet and hands. Wherever there was any feeling left, he ached.

His shoulders, especially, were throbbing with pain. The ache of the cold and the strain of supporting his body were beginning to tell. He felt that he could hold on no longer. It almost seemed attractive to slide into the smooth softness of the water and just drift away. With a start, he dismissed such thinking from his mind. He couldn't let go! He had to hold on!

"Heavenly Father," he prayed. "Please make them hurry! I don't think I can last much longer!"

It was then—just as Spindles was praying—that Lonely remembered the old feldspar mine. *I wonder if that's where he is?* he said to himself. *Could be! 'Sfull of water now. I wonder if he's fallen in!*

He revved his bike and raced to the mine, clattering over rocks and sliding through loose stones. He scratched himself on mulga branches and forged his way through thick spinifex, as high as his head, without even feeling the sharp pointed grass on his hands and face.

Soon he was in the foothills, near the mine, and then he was at the mine itself.

He knew how dangerous it was, and parked his bike well back from the edge. He examined the hard ground. To most people there was nothing to see. But his practised eye detected signs of recent movement. Loose stones that had been kicked. Grass freshly nibbled by a pony. Broken sticks.

He crawled past the notice that warned of danger and then saw the place where part of the edge had broken away.

As Spindles had done, he lay down on his stomach and looked over the edge.

In a moment he took in the whole scene. Long used to searching for lost sheep in the far corners of the huge outback station, he quickly saw Spindles' desperate position and instantly knew what to do.

"Spindles!" he shouted. "'Ang on, son. We'll 'ave you out of there in no time!"

Spindles heard the voice and looked up. No sound of magpie on a spring morning, or cool, running water on a blistering summer day could have been more sweet to his ears than Lonely's rough raucous "Spindles!"

"Lonely!" he called. "H-help m-me! H-help me out! Help me g-get out of here!"

And his voice choked up and tears gathered in his eyes.

But Lonely was already gone. The usually slow, quiet boundary rider seemed now like a darting goanna. In a flash, he had returned to his motorcycle, grabbed a rope, tied one end of it to a huge boulder about four metres from the edge of the mine and begun to lower himself over the edge of the cliff. The lip crumbled under the rope and clumps of dirt tumbled down, showering him with dust and grit. Soon however, the rope had bitten its way through to harder earth underneath and the fragmenting ceased.

Kicking his feet against the cliff wall to protect his face and hands from the rough earth he bounced his way down to the water.

Soon he had his strong arms around Spindles, and had lifted his shivering, wet form out of the water. He tied the end of the rope around Spindles' waist and sat him on the ledge where he had first stood to rescue his hat.

"Wait 'ere a minute, son," said Lonely, and began to climb back up, hand over hand, feet pressed against the mine wall until he reached the top.

"OK, Spins," he called and began to haul Spindles slowly up. The boy also used his feet to stop his body scraping against the rocky earth of the wall, but he was still so cold and stiff that he suffered many a scratch and bruise before he finally found himself safe in Lonely's arms.

Sleepy, normally as quiet and docile as his master, jumped up and down excitedly when he saw Spindles, and even barked once or twice, as he wagged his tail furiously in welcome.

Soon, Spindles was wrapped in Lonely's large coat, and sitting on the petrol tank of the bike, while they hastened back to the homestead.

The rest of you can imagine for yourself. How his mother wept with joy, and his father tried to calm her down; how Spindles seemed to be drinking warm drinks and having a hot bath and snuggling into a warm bed all at once; and then how he slept for a long time.

It was two weeks before he was out and about again. He had caught a very bad chill and it took some time to recover.

One day, the inevitable question had to be asked.

"Timothy, why did you climb over the edge?"

"Well, Dad, I dropped my hat in the mine and I thought Mum would be cross if I lost it so—"

"What were you doing so near the edge of the mine? Didn't you see the warning sign?"

"Well, yes, but I thought—"

"What do you mean, you *thought*? Why do you think I put the sign there in the first place?"

"*You* put it there, Dad? I didn't know you put it there."

"Yes, I put it there. I knew the mine was dangerous, and I didn't want anyone to be hurt. Particularly, you!"

"Golly, Dad, I should have realised there was some reason for it."

"Of course there was, you scatterbrain. Signs like that are not put there to make things difficult. They're for your protection because people care about silly fellows like you!"

When Spindles recovered, he made a special trip to see Redgum.

"Redgum," he began, "I've come to say I'm sorry."

As usual, Redgum waited quietly for him to continue.

"Redgum, you remember when I was complaining about people always telling me what to do? You said it was because they loved me. I think I know what you mean now.

"You know that sign near the old feldspar mine? Well that was put there for the same reason, I think. My dad said he did it because he cared about people—and me in particular.

"Is that why God gives us commandments too?"

The great Redgum tree stood silent for a moment.

Then he said, in his strong, firm, but loving voice, "Spindles, my son, I think you will find the best answer to your question in the Bible. When you go home tonight why don't you read this verse?—First John, chapter 5, verse 3."

"First John, chapter 5, verse 3," repeated Spindles. "Thank you, Redgum, I will!"

"He hurried home straight away, saying to himself, "First John, chapter 5, verse 3, First John, chapter 5, verse 3, First John . . ."

When he sat on his bed with his Bible open later on, this is what he read:

This is the love of God, that we keep his commandments. And his commandments are not burdensome.

So God gives us commandments because he loves us, too, Spindles said to himself. *And they are not too heavy to bear. I guess I'd better keep them then.*

And that is just what he tried to do.

4

Spindles and the Bushfire

Spindles was sitting on the edge of his bed, lost to the rest of the world.

Beside him was a little pile of strange and varied objects. He was gazing at it intently.

Then, slowly, he began to examine each article, one by one, naming each one as he did so, and carefully shifting it a few inches away, to start a new pile.

"String," he said quietly, and put it to one side. "Knife . . . hanky . . . paper clip . . . plastic horse . . . quartz crystal . . . creek-stone . . . model . . ." and they, too, were put to one side. He lingered a bit over the model, which was a piece of wood about three inches long carved into a shape which could have been the beginnings of either a submarine or a rocket or a crocodile, depending on your point of view.

He continued with the last few items. "Whistle . . . empty pill bottle . . . Pakistani stamp."

No matches.

He stood up, and reached his hands deep into his pockets. Then he slapped his sides, as if he was frisking himself. He stooped down and looked under the bed. He examined his chest of drawers, opening each drawer one by one. He even looked behind it.

Nowhere could he find his matches.

Not that the matches were of much value. But Spindles usually kept them in a special tin with a tightly fitting lid. The tin had originally contained cough lozenges, but most of the label had been scraped away by Spindles himself. For he had spent half an hour one day—when he should have been doing some study—painstakingly and artistically scratching his own name across the lid:

SPINDLES

The tin, of course, kept the matches dry if he happened to be playing in the creek or was caught in the rain. And in the bush, you should always carry matches. You never know when you might need them.

But he couldn't find the tin.

Oh well, he must have lost it somewhere. He would just have to get another one.

It was almost bed time now, so he opened

his Bible to read a few verses before he went
to sleep.

This is what he read:

Christ also suffered for you, leaving you an
example, that you should follow in his steps.
He committed no sin; no guile was found on
his lips. When he was reviled, he did not revile
in return; When he suffered, he did not
threaten; But he trusted to him who judges
justly. He himself bore our sins in his body on
the tree, that we might die to sin and live to
righteousness.
(1 Peter 2:21-24)

He thought about that for a while, and
realised how true it was. Jesus Christ had done
just that. He had not tried to defend himself.
He had not threatened his persecutors. For our
sake, he had been prepared to suffer.

The next day was very hot. It was a
scorcher. By nine o'clock, the sun was high in
the sky and the heat was oppressive. To walk
outside was to walk into an oven.

The house was built with wide verandahs
and large windows so that it was protected by
a wall of shade and any breeze could blow
right through. It was a little cooler inside.

But soon a hot wind sprang up and swept
across the yard and into the house itself,

bringing with it all the heat that it had scooped up from eight hundred kilometres of wide, flat, baking earth to the north.

The trees began to sway in the wind, their leaves streaming out sideways, roaring and bustling as they did. Swirls of dust sprang up, little willy-willies spinning their way past the house.

Spindles stretched out on the dining room floor, where the cold lino was pleasant at first. Soon, however, it became sticky and warm and he had to shift.

By lunch time, the heat had grown worse, and it was hard to become interested in anything.

Suddenly, there was a shout in the yard. Then the sound of running footsteps and doors banging.

Spindles sprang to his feet and raced outside. The heat wrapped itself around him like a thick blanket and he wished he could throw it off.

In the middle of the yard, the men were talking quickly and pointing to the north-east.

"Looks like it started at the top of the Range, Boss," Kamulla was saying.

"Just above the Opal Pool, I'd say," said Butch.

"Yes," said Mr. Thornton, "And if it has

started there, there's not a thing we can do about it. We'd never get in there now."

"Main thing is to save the house and the stock," added Butch.

Spindles looked over toward the Range. There, high above the top of the hills, was a tall, drifting column of grey smoke. It rose hundreds of metres into the air, well above the brown clouds of dust.

It was the thing that station owners and their families dreaded perhaps more than anything else—a bushfire!

"I think the homestead will probably be all right, judging by the direction of the wind," said Mr. Thornton. "But we'd better have someone stand by to open the yards and let the horses out if necessary, all the same."

"I reckon the creek might stop the fire from coming this way," said Lonely. "What do you think about driving down there and keeping watch?"

"Good idea," answered Mr. Thornton.

In a few moments, the men were crowded into the four-wheel drive vehicle and were bouncing their way to the creek. And Spindles was there, too, crammed into the back, where the hard metal floor and sides bruised and battered him as they raced over the rough track.

Soon they were at the creek. The fire had not reached the track, yet, but they could still see it greedily gulping its way down from the Range-top. Then great clouds of smoke rose up, hiding the fire, and Spindles could feel his eyes stinging. He coughed once or twice to clear his lungs of the choking fumes.

Suddenly, his heart gave a jump and his eyes widened. What about the animals? What about Redgum? He had been so taken up with the fire that he had forgotten all about them.

Now he was really worried. What if they were caught in the flames? What if they were killed? And what if Redgum was burned?

Spindles lost interest in what the men were doing or saying and desperately tried to peer through the smoke to see what was happening.

I wonder if I could cross the creek and help them? he thought. But he knew that his father would never allow it. Besides, what could he do? He might only lose his own life and that would just make things worse.

Then he saw the flames.

They were fierce and hot and racing toward the creek.

The spinifex grass crackled and exploded into flame so that the ground across the creek became a carpet of fire.

Then, a couple of kangaroos burst out of the smoke almost right in front of them, stopped for a moment in bewilderment at seeing the men and bounded off along the creek bed, to the south.

Overhead, galahs, cockatoos and parrots swarmed upwards, screeching and squawking, safe from the fire, but confused by the smoke and frightened by the heat.

"I wonder if Gleam is all right," muttered Spindles to himself.

Then, he stood awe-struck by the sight of a burst of flame shooting from the bottom to the top of a tree, consuming the leaves in an instant and then quietly settling down to the slower work of burning away at the smaller twigs and branches. Given enough time, the fire would eat its way into the trunk itself, destroying its inner life and leaving it blackened, broken and dead, only a poor memory of the majestic thing it had once been.

An emu shot out of the confusion of smoke and flame. In a moment it was lost again from view, but Spindles knew who it was.

"Hippie!" he said, excitedly. "Good on you, Hippie! You can beat it!"

"What did you say, son?" asked Spindles' father.

"Eh?" answered Spindles, turning round quickly. "Oh, nothing Dad."

His father was watching the fire very closely and did not bother to find out any more.

Meanwhile Spindles kept on looking. What about Roo, and Joey, and Tank, and Bilby? Would they be safe? If only he could see them, or talk to them.

Through the smoke he imagined he could see a low grey shape darting across the ground and heading for the creek bed. But he was not sure. If only the smoke would clear! It might have been Tank!

But now Spindles' attention was focussed on something else. Small flames were beginning to lick around the base of the great Redgum tree! Soon larger flames would be trying to take hold of the bark, slither up to the branches, devour the leaves, and feast on the twigs.

"Please, God, don't let Redgum be burned!" Spindles prayed quickly, but he kept his eyes open, fearing to stop looking for an instant.

The men had other problems, for the fire was right at the edge of the creek and threatening to jump across. The creek bed was quite dry, and there were patches of dry bark, driftwood, leaves and grass scattered over it. Otherwise, there were stones—thousands of them, laid out thickly like a cobbled road. And they would never burn.

Butch was in the middle of the creek bed with a large bag, beating at the small fire that had started in a patch of leaves and bark.

Mr. Thornton was applying a tiny, feeble stream of water from his knapsack spray to another small fire.

Lonely was dragging a few larger pieces of wood apart so that the fire could not get hold of them all together.

But Spindles saw none of that. His attention was riveted on Redgum.

A great struggle was taking place. Redgum, somehow, stood taller and stronger than Spindles had ever seen before. It was as if he was rising above the flames, defying them, daring them to attack.

And the fire was like a pack of angry, hungry dogs, leaping and snarling and mouthing at the tree, yet unable to get hold of it.

The fire seemed to know that its time was limited. Soon the grass would be consumed and the flames would die down. If it was going to take the tree, it would have to do it now. Several large, vivid flames rose up, up, almost to the lowest of Redgum's strong, overhanging branches.

The tips of the flames met the tips of the leaves. For a moment, the two faced each other, until the leaves began to curl upwards, drying and dying as they did.

A shudder passed through the tree, as if of pain.

Exalted with their victory, the flames rose higher again, reaching, grasping, biting, clutching, using every resource to gain a death-grip on the tree.

Pieces of bark on the lower trunk grew black and crisp. Dried leaves began to break off in the wind and whip away into the dusty smoke clouds.

Indeed, the wind conspired with the fire to attack the tree, for just when it seemed that the flames might die away again, gusts of wind urged them into anger and they renewed the attack.

Again, they leapt up toward Redgum's branches. Again, some of the leaves crackled, flared and died. Now, the bark on the lowest and largest overhanging branch began to smoulder and glow. Soon, it would be alight.

Meanwhile, the ring of fire surrounding the base of the trunk continued its slow, persistent, gnawing, its flame-teeth stripping away the outer layers and probing longingly for the deep, inner wood, where it could devour the Redgum's heart.

Again, a great, trembling shudder took hold of the tree. The upper branches shook and rattled, the leaves scraping together and whispering their agony. Even the roots quivered in the ground.

Spindles was terrified. What would he do if Redgum were burned? Who else could teach him the things that Redgum could teach? Indeed, how would the creatures of the Dusty Range exist without the wisdom of the great tree to guide them?

Then, something happened that Spindles saw, and yet did not see. Afterwards, looking back on it, he could not have told you what was different. Yet something was different. A change came over Redgum and a change came over the fire.

In some mysterious way, the tree's presence increased. It was the same tree, and it was the same size that it had always been. But there was more of it—it was present in a way that Spindles had never seen. Redgum filled Spindles' whole vision. There was nothing else there but the tree and the fire. All else—animals, trees, smoke, people—might as well have not existed.

And the flames retreated. Like a beaten dog, they cowed and whimpered away, turning two or three times, but seeing the tree and grovelling and scraping down and away again.

Redgum's deep roots, hard wood and inner strength had defeated the fire!

The crisis was past and the fire now left the Range and wandered out into the flat country. Here it slowed down and lost itself not knowing where to go, until it finally petered out and died in the desert.

It had not crossed the creek, and the homestead was safe.

That night at the dinner table, there was much talk about the fire, of course. How it started, how far it had burned, what damage it had done, whether the country would regenerate and so on.

Generally, it was agreed that no stock had been lost nor fences damaged, and that in a few months, you would never know that there had been a fire at all.

But Spindles was still anxious and worried. What had happened to his friends? Were they still alive? Would they ever meet again? He longed to find out.

The next day, he hurried to the creek, and raced to Redgum.

"Redgum, are you all right?" he asked excitedly.

"What do you think?" replied Redgum, smiling. "Of course, I'm all right!"

"I'm glad to hear that," answered Spindles. "What about Hippie, and Roo and Joey and—"

"Why don't you go and ask them yourself?" said Redgum.

So Spindles knew straight away that they were all safe and ran off to find them.

Hippie was the first one he saw.

"Hippie!" he shouted. "I knew you'd be all right. I knew you could do it!"

"Of course," answered Hippie stiffly. "But what do you mean, you knew I could do it. What did you know?"

"Well, I saw you run in front of the fire yesterday. I knew you'd escape."

"So you *were* there, after all?" answered Hippie, with a strange emphasis on the word "were."

"I don't follow you, Hippie," answered Spindles. "I was there with my dad to see if we could stop the fire crossing the creek."

"You knew all about it then?"

"We saw it—from the homestead, and we drove over," said Spindles, puzzled by Hippie's strange behaviour.

"What's the matter with you, Hippie?" he asked. "What are you getting at?"

"How did the fire start, Spindles?"

"How would I know?"

"Are you sure you weren't there when it started?"

"Me? No. I don't even know where it started. I was home yesterday. It was too hot to be out anyway."

"Well, what about this, then?"

And Hippie held out to Spindles the lid of a

tin. It was an old cough lozenge tin. And scratched on to the lid was the name:

SPINDLES

"My match tin!" exclaimed Spindles, taking it in his hand. "Where did you get it? I've been looking everywhere for it."

"I'm sure you have," said Hippie coldly. "You wouldn't want anyone to know where you left it."

"Hippie, what are you talking about?" Spindles asked, now really perplexed. "If I knew where I left it, I wouldn't have lost it, would I?"

"You know where you left it, all right, old chap. Right where the fire started."

Suddenly Spindles realised what Hippie was getting at.

"Hippie, you don't think that—that I—that I started the fire, do you?"

Hippie was silent.

"Hippie, answer me. Do you really think that?"

"Well, that's where the tin was found, Spins," said Hippie, sullenly. "It adds up, doesn't it? A bushfire starts and your match tin is found right where it starts. You have to admit, old chap, that it looks rather bad for you."

"Who found the tin, Hippie? Did you?"

"Well, no, actually, I didn't. Koorook found it."

"Koorook! I didn't know he was a friend of yours. How long since you've associated with crows?"

"Now, be fair, old chap. Play the game. You know jolly well that Koorook is not my friend."

"Well, how did you come by this lid?"

"Actually, Spins, Gleam gave it to me."

"You said you got it from Koorook."

"No, I didn't. Koorook found it. He gave it to Gleam and Gleam gave it to me. And Koorook told Gleam that he saw you light a fire."

"Me? Light a fire? In the middle of summer? I know I do some silly things sometimes, but I'm not that silly. Dad would murder me. What else did the old crow say?"

"He said that yesterday he was sitting in a tree at the head of the gorge when he saw you come along. Then, you sat down in a clear spot under a few rocks, where no one could see you, and started playing with your matches. You had made a circle of grass and were trying to make the fire follow the circle round.

"Then, you left the matches there and wandered off in another direction, intending to return, no doubt. Meanwhile, a bit of a wind sprang up and the smouldering grass was blown on to some spinifex—and then the fire started."

"But Hippie, you know I wouldn't do that!"

"Well, Spins, I don't know. You climbed a cliff when you weren't equipped for it. You went off without snake wire one day. Then you fell into the feldspar mine. And you rode your bike the morning you got it before you were supposed to. And . . ."

"All right, Hippie. I know. I guess I do get into trouble pretty easily. Starting a fire like that is the sort of thing I would do. But I didn't, Hippie. I didn't!"

"Well, I'd like to believe you, Spins. But, Koorook did find the lid, and, well, it's jolly hard to know what to believe".

Just then, Gleam appeared flying overhead.

"Hey, Gleam!" Spindles called.

But Gleam kept flying.

Spindles was both hurt and astonished.

He wandered away from Hippie, and although the emu felt sorry for Spindles, it did seem as though Spindles was responsible. So he let him go.

Spindles was angry. Didn't even his friends trust him?

But after a while he calmed down. He *was* a bit of a scatterbrain at times. And he couldn't really blame the others for being suspicious.

As he wandered on, he saw Tank sunning himself on a rock. He walked quietly over.

"Morning, Tank," he said half-heartedly.

"Oh," said the goanna, looking up. "It's you."

"That's not very polite, Tank," said Spindles.

"Well, lighting a fire and leaving it is not very bright either," said Tank.

So Tank knew the story, too. Apparently everyone did!

"'Ave a look around you, son," said Tank, gruffly. "Look! Black. Everything black as a midnight sky. No grass. 'Alf the trees dead. The scrub all gone. And worst of all, a couple of my friends gone, too. It's no joke, Spins."

"A couple of your friends, Tank? Burned?" Tank nodded slightly.

"Oh, Tank, I'm sorry. That's awful."

"Pretty big price to pay for a bit of carelessness," answered Tank, and then slipped off the rock and disappeared up the creek.

Spindles was now really upset. He could understand Tank being distressed. But it wasn't his fault. He hadn't started the fire. Why did that old crow say he did?

Spindles never had much to do with Koorook. Not that anyone did for that matter. He was a mean bird and seemed to like making mischief. That's why he found it hard to understand why the others believed him.

How easily people seem to believe the worst about you, thought Spindles. *Even if you do deserve it sometimes!*

Just then, he heard a movement in a nearby tree.

There, sitting on a low branch, was Koorook, his black feathers invisible against the burnt wood. Slowly, he flapped his large wings, and without a sound, rose into the air, casually lifting himself above the cliff and out of sight. Just as he disappeared, Spindles heard his drawn-out moaning cry. And he could still picture the evil gleam in Koorook's eye as he flew away.

Spindles wandered back toward the Redgum Tree. Suddenly, he noticed Joey hopping toward him.

"G'day, Joey," he said sullenly. He kept going, his hands in his pockets, one hand holding the lid of the match tin, and kicking at the burnt ground as he walked.

"Stop a minute, Spins," said Joey.

"What for?" asked Spindles. "Do you want to tell me that you think I did it, too?"

"No," answered Joey. "I don't."

Spindles stopped. Perhaps Joey believed in him anyway. Or maybe he hadn't heard the story.

"Spindles," Joey began, and then hesitated. He tried again. "Spindles, I've got to tell you something."

"Well, go on, then," said Spindles testily.

"About the fire, Spins. I know you didn't do it."

"Oh? How do you know?"

"Well, I know, because, because—well, because, I did!"

"You did? What do you mean, Joey?"

"Well, what I mean is, I lit the fire."

"You lit it, Joey? You? How could you light a fire?"

"You remember how last weekend you were poking around with me at the top of the gorge?"

"Yes."

"Well, you dropped your matches out of your pocket. Yesterday, I was up there by myself, and found them. I decided to see if I could light one.

"So I opened the tin—which was hard work; it's a pretty tight lid—then I tried to strike a match. The first couple wouldn't work at all. They kept breaking."

"You probably held them too near the end," explained Spindles.

"Well, the next one, I held closer. Then suddenly it came alight. It burned my hand, and I got such a shock I dropped it. It landed in a patch of spinifex and—well you can guess the rest."

Joey held his head down shamefully.

"And now everyone's blaming me!" said Spindles angrily.

"I'm sorry, Spins. I really am. That's why I owned up."

"Well, that's something, I suppose. But what about everyone else? They still think I did it!"

He looked hard at Joey. Joey knew what he was thinking.

"Spins, do you want me to tell all the others too?"

"Well, it would be a help," he remarked.

Then something happened that Spindles never did quite understand. Suddenly into his mind came the words of his Bible reading of two days before.

"Christ also suffered for you, leaving you an example, that you should follow in his steps . . . When he was reviled, he did not revile in return; when he suffered he did not threaten; but he trusted to him who judges justly."

When Jesus had been falsely accused, he had not tried to justify himself or shift the blame. He had willingly accepted it that we might go free. He had taken the guilt of our sin so that we might not have to bear it. And he had left us an example.

Suddenly Spindles saw another possibility.

Why not let people go on believing that he had started the fire? Then Joey would not have to suffer. And as he looked at Joey, he realised how hard it had been for him to own up, and how hard it would be for him to have to own up to everyone else.

But then, he realised how hard it would be for him, too, if he went on letting people feel he was guilty!

What should he do? He would ask Redgum. He would know.

"Hang on, Joey!" he said, and scampered toward the tree.

He skidded to a stop in front of Redgum.

"Redgum, I've got a problem. All the others think that—"

"I know, I know," said Redgum kindly.

"Yes, I suppose you do," said Spindles.

"But I've just found out something, Redgum. Joey says that he did it!"

"I know that too."

"Oh," said Spindles. "Well, Redgum, what should I do about it? I've been thinking about what Jesus did. I don't want to take the blame for something I didn't do, but if I do let everyone go on thinking I did it, it will save Joey from getting into trouble.

"One part of me says to make Joey own up and the other part says not to. What should I do? Should I make him tell? Or do I have to cover up for him?"

"You don't *have* to do anything, Spindles," answered Redgum. "The whole question is

very simple, really. It all depends on how much you love Joey."

Spindles looked at Redgum. Then he turned and looked at the lonely, frightened little figure of Joey sitting dejectedly some distance away.

And he knew that even if the others never spoke to him again, there was only one thing he could do.

That night, as he lay in bed, he had mixed feelings. He was still hurt that his friends doubted his word.

But then he remembered the look of relief that had come over Joey when he learned what Spindles had decided to do.

And a deep sense of peace and contentment came over him.

Redgum was right.

When you love someone, it does make a difference!

5

Spindles and the Eagles

"Timothy! Come back here!"

It was Spindles' mother calling.

"Have you washed your face and cleaned your teeth?"

"No, Mum," said Spindles wearily.

He walked back inside, scuffing his feet on the lino as he did so.

"And don't scrape your feet!" his mum went on. "Do you want me to spend all day scrubbing floors?"

"No, Mum," answered Spindles again.

He made his way to the bathroom and picked up the facewasher. It was faintly damp, so he rubbed it across his cheeks and mouth, carefully avoiding his eyes.

"Well, that's my face washed," he said.

He picked up his toothbrush and squeezed toothpaste on to it. But he squeezed too hard, and the toothpaste fell over the end of the brush on to the floor. So he had to wipe that up. He used the facewasher. He brushed his teeth three or four times, dropped his toothbrush, still half full of toothpaste, into the wash basin, and wandered out again.

He was almost out the door, when his mother spotted him. "Let me see," she demanded, grasping him by the shoulders. She looked briefly at his face, then at his teeth. "Go back and do the job properly," she ordered.

"Yes, Mum," said Spindles, now resigned to the task, and retraced his steps slowly to the bathroom.

The facewasher still had dirt on it, so by the time he had rinsed it out a bit, washed his face "properly" and cleaned his teeth again, it seemed that half the day was gone.

Spindles had been in trouble all morning. At the breakfast table, he had tipped his milk drink on to his toast. Some of it had dribbled to the floor. Then he had been reprimanded for not making his bed. And he had forgotten to change into clean clothes. And he had not polished his shoes. And now he had been made to wash his face and brush his teeth twice.

Spindles was not very happy.

Anyway, it was Saturday. Why couldn't he have Saturday off from work? It wasn't fair.

He saddled his pony and rode off at full

speed to the Range. The poor pony did not know what was going on. Spindles was usually very kind to him, but now he was digging his heels into his side, and even hitting him around the ears with the end of the rein.

By the time Spindles arrived at the creek, he had calmed down a bit, but he was still very sour.

"What's wrong with you?" asked Joey.

"Everything!" answered Spindles. And he proceeded to tell Joey about the harsh treatment he had received.

"It doesn't sound very harsh to me," Joey commented.

"That's all right about you!" Spindles retorted. "You don't have to make *your* bed, or polish *your* shoes, or clean *your* teeth, or wash *your* face! I do, and I don't like it. It's just a waste of time, that's all! I hate it."

The great Redgum tree was standing silently by while this conversation was going on. He spoke now, quietly. And was there the faintest twinkle in his eye as he did?

"It all depends on your point of view," he murmured. "You're looking at things the wrong way up."

"And what's that supposed to mean?" answered Spindles angrily.

Joey was horrified. No one ever spoke to

Redgum like that! He stood back petrified, wondering what Redgum would say. But Redgum said nothing.

Spindles realised now what he had done. He backed off slowly, keeping his eyes to the ground. He banged into the pony, turned, jumped on and rode up the gorge toward the hills.

Now he was really in a mess. He had argued with his mother, and his friend Joey, and now, with Redgum. But it wasn't fair, anyway. They had no right to gang up on him like that!

Spindles was so wrapped up in his own problems that he didn't realise at first that none of his friends were nearby. They had all found something else to do.

No one enjoys being with a grouch.

About an hour later, Spindles found himself in a part of the Range that he rarely visited. He had been so angry inside that he hadn't taken much notice of where he was going.

Now he was right at the top of a ridge. Down to his left he became aware of a very narrow gorge that he hadn't ever visited before. It was only a few feet wide at the head, but it began sharply, not gradually, as most of them do.

He dismounted and walked to the edge. Beneath him were sheer cliffs dropping down about ten metres. He was at the point of a huge V, that opened up slowly and stretched away from him. Further out, the gorge was about 60 metres wide, and just as deep.

But what interested Spindles was the fact that the bottom of the gorge was strewn with huge boulders. Some of them were as big as his bedroom! It looked as though the cliffs had actually broken away, and tumbled into the gorge. In fact, you could almost imagine a giant pair of hands holding a huge hammer and chisel and chipping the cliffs away until the fragments fell below. But what fragments! Bigger than any rocks Spindles had seen before.

As he looked down on them, he began to imagine what it would be like climbing over them.

I wonder if I could get down there? he mused. He lay down on his stomach and looked over the edge. Beneath him it was very steep, but further around to his right, there seemed to be an area that was broken and rugged. It might be possible to climb down there.

He edged his way around and started to pick his way down. He found that the climb was not too difficult. It was certainly not as dangerous as the climb he had made in the

Dusty Range Creek when he had become stranded half-way up.

He found hand and footholds that were easy and safe to use. Soon he was almost at the bottom.

He jumped lightly from the cliff face to the top of a large boulder. He jumped down again on to another big rock. Then he jumped again.

Each of the boulders was as big as a toolshed. Some of them were three to four metres high. It was fun jumping from one to another.

Joey would have no trouble with this, Spindles thought. *Neither would Tank. Poor old Hippie wouldn't get on too well, though.* And at the thought of Hippie trying to leap among these boulders, he laughed outright. He pictured the large emu trying to manage the slippery rock surfaces with his clumsy feet and long, clawed toes. They would slither all over the place. Hippie would tumble and slide in an awkward tangle like a feather duster with three handles, all pointing in different directions!

And then he remembered how rude he had been to everyone that morning and he was sorry. It was fun exploring his new canyon, but it would have been more fun with somebody with him.

Spindles was now standing on a very large

chunk of rock. He looked up at the cliff face. He fancied he could see the very spot that this boulder had broken away from. Then he looked below him. About three metres down was another rock, with a fairly flat surface. He was sure he could jump that far.

So he sprang down.

Three metres is a long way when you're a small boy. And rock is much harder than your bed or the sand that lies in a dry gorge.

Spindles landed with a jar. Although he flexed his knees to allow for the hardness of the rock, it was not enough. His left foot twisted and he cried out for pain.

He overbalanced, falling to the edge of the boulder. Frantically he grabbed for something to hold on to. There was nothing.

He rolled over the edge and like a bale of hay being thrown from a truck, tumbled to the next rock a few feet further down. The breath thumped from his body as he landed. And then he cracked the back of his head and knew no more.

His body slid from the rock, and fell into a crevice between the boulders. Here there was a little grass, a few broken sticks and small stones. A native palm bush of some kind spread its fronds over Spindles' body.

It was some time before Spindles regained consciousness.

The sun had continued its relentless path across the sky. A few clouds nervously crept over the hill tops to look down into the valley. The wind dropped and all was still.

Spindles' eyes slowly opened. At first, everything was blurred, and the sunlight hurt his eyes. After a few minutes, however, he could look around. He had a headache and his ankle was very painful. He tried to climb to his feet, but as soon as he put any pressure on his left foot, he winced with the pain.

A cold chill of fear gripped his heart. He looked up through the palm fronds, over the boulders, to the gorge top. There was no way he could climb out of there now.

He was stranded!

And he was alone!

He sat down again, his thoughts in a turmoil.

What could he do?

How would he ever get out?

Who would even know where he was?

If only he hadn't been so foolish and grumpy this morning. Then it would never have happened!

Two tears welled up in Spindles' eyes and slowly slid down his cheeks, leaving little shiny paths through the dust and freckles. Then there were more, one after the other, and he was soon weeping aloud. What would happen to him! Perhaps he would die there! He might never again see his family or his friends. Even the thought of cleaning his teeth and making his bed didn't seem too bad any more when compared with the warmth of his mother's love and the security of his home.

Spindles became aware of a drop in temperature. He began to shiver, both with weeping and with cold. The sun had passed beyond the brink of the cliff, and deep, long shadows were reaching out over the valley floor, covering the boulders like a spidery, grey blanket.

Now, Spindles was really frightened, for he knew how cold it could get in the Outback at night time. And although it was still only afternoon, the heat was already fading away.

He sniffed and hugged himself, trying to keep warm, racking his brains to think of some way he could get out. This was the worst predicament he had ever been in.

Suddenly the whole sky was cut off by a heavier shadow.

Spindles looked up quickly and his breath caught in his mouth. There was a rush of wind, a whirr of wings, a sound of beating and above him, on either side of him, completely cutting off the blue sky, were two of the biggest wedgetail eagles he had ever seen in all his life.

If he had been frightened before, he was terrified now! The situation had been desperate enough. Now it was doubly so. The tears evaporated in a moment. His lips were dry. His eyes opened wide in awe. He tried to cry out but the words stuck in his throat, and only a croaking whisper emerged.

The two eagles settled on the rock above him. He crouched in the crevice between them, like a furtive rabbit, desperate, but not knowing where to go or what to do.

One of the eagles, the smaller one, stretched out its huge wings. Spindles gazed at him, wide-eyed. Those wings seemed to reach out forever. Each one must have been as long as he was. Probably three metres from tip to tip. And if the other eagle was larger again . . .? The thought was almost too much to handle.

Any moment, Spindles expected the eagles to pounce on him and start tearing him from limb to limb.

What did happen took Spindles completely by surprise. The eagle who had spread his wings spoke to him. In a voice that reminded him of Redgum's, although it was really very different, more high pitched, and sharper somehow, the eagle said firmly, "Don't be afraid. There is nothing to fear."

At last Spindles found his voice. "D-don't be

af-fr-fraid?" he stammered. "Of-of eagles? Don't eagles kill sheep, and—and rabbits, and—" He paused, trying to collect his thoughts.

"My dad says that eagles take baby lambs from the flock and—"

The eagle cut him off. "Sometimes," he said. "It is necessary for a lamb to die in order that we might live. But you have no need to fear. We will not hurt you."

Spindles looked at the two birds suspiciously. He saw their gleaming eyes, and their cruel, curved beaks. He thought of their pointed claws. He didn't know whether to believe them or not. But the first eagle was still speaking.

"Let me introduce myself," he suggested politely. "My name is Krag. This is my mate Bigi."

Bigi nodded her head slightly.

"We have come to help you. We will get you out of here."

Now Spindles was really confused. Eagles wanting to help him?

"What do you mean?" he managed to say softly.

"We will lift you out of here as if you were a lamb and fly you to safety," said Krag.

A spark of hope leapt into Spindles' heart. He thought of home, and his parents, who loved him, and his friends, and Redgum. He would see them again after all. Then he thought of being lifted into the air by an eagle! And he was afraid again. What if they only wanted to lift him up in order to drop him and kill him and feed on him like a rabbit or a dingo pup? It was probably a trap, a cruel trick to make fun of him.

"What do you mean, fly me out of here?" he asked cautiously. "How can you do that? I'm a lot heavier than a lamb."

"We will both lift you together," answered Krag. "Bigi will take your feet and I will take your shoulders and we will fly you out."

"How can you do that? What if you both try to fly different directions at once? I've never heard of two eagles carrying something together!" Spindles argued.

"Team work," Krag answered simply. "It's amazing what you can do when you work together with someone. Two together can do far more than the same two can ever do separately."

"Well, how do I know you won't just drop me when we get a few feet up?" Spindles replied, not knowing whether to believe them or not.

"I'm afraid you don't," answered Krag. "That is a risk you must take. The only way you will know is to let us try it. You must trust us."

Spindles was still a bit groggy from his fall, but he knew exactly what was being asked of him. *If I let them try it,* he thought, *I might get home tonight. Or I might be smashed on the rocks. Even if they mean it, it might be too much for them. They might even drop me without meaning to.*

Then he thought of what would happen if he said no. He would probably freeze to death . . . or die of exposure . . . or hunger and thirst. . . . no one would ever find him. No one knew where he was.

I wish I knew what to do. I wish there was someone who could help me, he thought. *God,* he prayed silently, *What shall I do?*

Then Bigi spoke. "Spindles," she said.

She used my name, thought Spindles. *How did she know?*

"Spindles," said Bigi. "The only way you can escape is by faith. Won't you trust us?"

And now Spindles thought he heard something in Bigi's voice that reminded him of Redgum. His voice was deep and strong; hers was thin, and high pitched. But somewhere, somehow, there was something true about it.

"All right," he whispered fearfully. "I will do it."

"Then lie still," Krag ordered. "We will come down to you."

The two great wedgetail eagles dropped down from the rocks into the crevice. Bigi landed at his feet. Krag actually landed on Spindles' shoulders, with one great leg planted either side of his head.

Spindles sat petrified. But he was all right. He was not hurt.

"Relax," said Bigi. "Everything will be all right."

Bigi then placed her strong feet on Spindles' calves and gripped them firmly. Spindles was surprised that the claws did not hurt. (*Perhaps they're like cats' claws,* he thought. *They only dig in if they want them to.*)

Then Krag gripped Spindles' upper arms. "Put your hands around my legs," he said. Spindles did.

"Here we go," called Krag. "Hang on tight."

There was a great thrashing of wings. Spindles closed his eyes as the great feathers beat all round his head. There was a rush of air, and suddenly he realised that he was no longer on the ground.

They hovered a few feet up, the large wings steadily beating. Spindles looked down over his shoulders. Below him were the solid rocks over which he had climbed. He turned away and closed his eyes tight. He couldn't look at them.

Slowly they continued to rise.

It was not easy, for the gorge was still not very wide at that point and the air currents were uncertain. Once, they all dropped suddenly for about two metres. *My fears were right!* Spindles thought. *They are going to let me go!* But both the birds held him firmly in their grasp and steadily made their way upwards again.

They were ten metres up now. Then fifteen. Then twenty. Now they were level with the tops of the cliffs. Now Spindles really began to believe what the eagles told him. They did want to save him after all!

And then they were up and away, soaring over the hilltops, riding over the mountains. The broad winds of the open sky carried them, like a huge box kite, up into the blue. Neither of the eagles now moved his wings much. They angled them to catch the direction of the wind and floated like corks on a calm sea.

Spindles looked down again. Below him lay the wrinkled Dusty Range, like the rugs of a large bed, untidily folded. Among those rough folds was the gorge in which a few minutes ago, he had lain, in fear of his life. The huge boulders there were now like small stones that he could pick up with two fingers and flick away. As they flew higher and further, the gorge became just a thin blue line drawn across the blanket of the Range. In fact, already, it was difficult to remember what it had been like to lie there in fear for his life. Looking down on it now, it seemed so small and so insignificant.

Spindles was really enjoying his flight. He was exhilarated! Thrilled! Delighted! Never in his life had he had such an adventure! "It must be fantastic to be able to fly like this!" he called to Krag. But the huge wedgetail could not hear him and gave no answer.

Soon they were over the Range and descending toward the homestead. Spindles peered down over his shoulder again. His hands were becoming tired now, for although he was not really taking any weight—Krag and Bigi were doing that—he was still holding as tight as he could and his muscles were feeling the strain.

"There's my pony!" he said suddenly. Again, neither eagle answered, but he was excited to see that his pony had wandered home and was just a few hundred metres from the gate.

Slowly and smoothly the eagles drifted toward the ground. They hovered just above the pony and then gently lowered Spindles down alongside of him. Their huge wings braced strongly as they descended the last metre or so and again Spindles closed his eyes.

When he felt the hard ground under him
again, he let go of Krag's legs. Before he knew
what was happening, the two birds
immediately shot into the air and catching a
gust of wind, streamed into the sky.

Spindles watched them go. Up, up they
went, like dark rockets, and soon they were
just black specks woven into the tapestry of
the sky.

"They didn't even wait to be thanked,"
Spindles said to himself in amazement.

His pony was standing quietly next to him,
apparently quite unmoved by the strange sight
of two eagles depositing his master on the
ground right before his eyes.

Spindles grabbed hold of the stirrup, and
standing on one foot, hauled himself into an
upright position. He caught hold of his horse's
mane, and taking all his weight that way, he
was able to put his good foot in the stirrup.
Then he hauled himself into the saddle and
rode the last few hundred metres to the house.

The sun was setting now and shadows were
stretching themselves out for the night. The
evening stillness could almost be felt as the
winds died away and the leaves of the mulga
trees by the track hung perfectly still.

The light from the windows was glowing
now and he could see smoke rising slowly

from the chimney. Spindles' mother was waiting at the door.

"Where have you been?" she demanded. "Your father and I have been worried about you. We were almost ready to send out a search."

Spindles remembered where he had been, and knew that they would never have found him in the dark. He shuddered.

He showed his mother his swollen ankle and she forgot all about her questions while she hurried him inside and cared for him.

"How did it happen?" she asked later.

"Oh, I was climbing some rocks and I fell off," he replied. "Then a couple of eagles came and I held on to their legs and they flew me back to—"

"Eagles!" exclaimed his mum. "What are you talking about, Timothy? You say the strangest things sometimes. You know very well that you came home on your pony."

"Yes, but—"

"Now, no more buts," said his mother.

So Spindles said no more.

But sitting in his hot bath that night, he thought how good it was to be in the warmth and comfort of his home. Much better than that cold, harsh gorge.

Then he remembered how small everything

had looked from the sky. He thought with pleasure of the flight with the eagles. He closed his eyes and saw it all again.

How different problems looked when you rose above them! It all depended on your point of view. You had to look at things from the right way up.

That night he opened his Bible and this is what he read:

He gives power to the faint,
and to him who has no might he increases strength.
Even youths shall faint and be weary, and young men shall fall exhausted;
But they who wait for the Lord shall renew their strength,
They shall mount up with wings like eagles.
(Isaiah 40:29-31)

I must remember that, he said to himself. *Next time things go wrong, I must try to get above them instead of letting them get on top of me.*

And he realised that with the help of the Lord, he could do it.

"I'm sorry about this morning," he said to the Lord. "Next time, I'll try to act better. And I'll try to have more faith in you to help me."

The next morning, two things happened that were interesting.

First of all, when Mum said to him, "Seeing you have hurt your leg, you needn't make your bed this morning, Timothy." Spindles answered brightly. "But I already have, Mum."

His mother looked at him with amazement. "Well, you *can* comb your hair and clean . . ." her voice faded away. Spindles' hair *was* combed. His face *was* clean. He was smiling at her with a cheesy grin, so that all his teeth were visible. They shone!

"Well! So you have already done that too. That's a pleasant change."

Spindles limped outside with the aid of a stick.

Then the second thing happened.

"G'day, young whippersnapper," called Butch. "'Ow's yer foot?"

"It's all right," answered Spindles. "I'll be able to walk on it soon."

They talked for a while. Then Butch happened to say, "Tell you what son, I saw a couple of beaut eagles yesterday. Right near the 'omestead. Biggest ones I've ever seen. I raced inside for me rifle but they were too far off by the time I got back. I reckon one of 'em 'as a four metre wing span."

"Nearer three," said Spindles.

"Eh?" said the stockman. "'Ow do you know? Did you see 'em too?"

"You'd be surprised," said Spindles.

Then he just sat there with a faraway look in his eyes.

And over the Dusty Range, the old Redgum Tree smiled to himself.

He knew now that Spindles understood.

6

Spindles and the Tom Cat

As soon as Spindles arrived at the Dusty Range creek, he knew that something was wrong.

He jumped down from his pony and stood listening. What was it? Everything *looked* the same. The sky was clear and blue as usual. The breeze was fresh and cool as usual. Redgum stood still in his usual place, quiet and grand. In the distance, Hippie was standing near some scraggy sprawling mallee, and Roo and Joey were feeding in the shade of some sugarwood.

But there was something out of place. Suddenly he realised what it was. He couldn't hear any birds. Not one. No magpie warbling. No cockatoo or galah screeching. No willy wagtail whistling. Nothing. Just silence.

He spotted Tank sunning himself on the grey, warm, dry trunk of a dead tree—a tree which had once stood strong and tall, like Redgum, but which now lay peacefully on its

side, its bark stripped and its sun-bleached timber smooth and clean, except for an occasional sharp point that neither goanna, nor bird nor wind nor rain had smoothed away. "Tank!" called Spindles.

The goanna lifted one eyelid but otherwise remained as motionless as the log on which he lay.

"Tank! What's happened to the birds?" Spindles asked.

"G'day, Spins," said Tank, in his slow outback drawl. "What birds?"

"All the birds," answered Spindles. "I can't hear a single one."

"Oh, they're all around 'ere, somewhere," said Tank. "They're just keeping quiet, that's all."

"Why?"

"I'll show you," said Tank. Then, like a great, grey piece of bark peeling from the dead tree, he slipped to the ground and glided across an open patch of earth to the foot of a smaller redgum.

Spindles found it a bit hard not to talk to every redgum he came across, but he knew that it was pointless. There was only one Redgum who spoke—and only one who listened, too, for that matter.

At the foot of the tree lay a few pink, grey and white feathers.

"Look," said Tank quietly.

"All I can see is some feathers," said Spindles.

"'Ow did they get there, mutton head?" asked Tank.

"How should I know?" asked Spindles. "A galah lost them, I suppose."

"More than lost 'em," said Tank, quietly. "That's all that's left of the galah that lost 'em. He's dead. Finished. Done for."

"How?" asked Spindles.

"'Ave you ever seen what a cat does to a bird when it catches one?" asked Tank.

"No, I haven't," answered Spindles. "My dad never lets any cats stay around our place at all."

"Well, there's one 'ere now, alright," said Tank. "And this is one poor galah you'll never see around 'ere again. A cat eats everything—body, wings, head—the lot. Except for a few feathers, of course."

"How could a cat get here?" asked Spindles. "Where would it come from?"

While they had been talking, Hippie had wandered over toward them.

"Probably a feral cat, old chap," he said.

"What's a feral cat?" Spindles asked, forgetting even to say, "Hello," although it was the first time he had seen Hippie that day.

"A tame cat that has gone wild," said Hippie. "Probably, some city people had a cat they didn't want, brought it with them on a drive one day and dropped it out of the car to fend for itself."

"Better if they'd drowned the thing," growled Tank.

"Absolutely, I quite agree!" said Hippie. "But they obviously didn't and now we have a rather sticky problem, what!"

Suddenly Spindles had a terrible thought that made him shudder all over.

"Tank . . . Hippie . . . this bird that the cat killed. It wasn't . . . it wasn't Gleam, was it?"

"Good heavens, no!" said Hippie.

"Strike, no!" said Tank at the same time. "I wouldn't 'ave been lying around in the sun dreaming if it had been!"

"But that's why Gleam's not around, old chap," Hippie explained.

"He and the other birds are rather shocked so they're keeping quiet for a while and staying up higher in the Range."

"Gleam, quiet?" asked Spindles in amazement. "I don't believe it!"

The other two laughed with Spindles. It was rather a rare event, you had to agree.

"What are we going to do?" asked Spindles.

"What do you mean, 'What are we goin' to

do'?" asked Tank. "What can we do about a wild tom cat?"

"There must be something," said Spindles.

"It's pretty hard to catch a cat, old chap," said Hippie. "Cats are quiet, fast and deadly. They can climb trees. They can see in the dark. They are quicker than a goanna—"

"'Ang on," said Tank. "Don't take things too far!"

"Oh, terribly sorry, Tank," said Hippie. "Almost as quick as a goanna—and as cruel as—as—well, as a cat! How can you catch a creature like that?"

Spindles wandered over to the Redgum tree. He held one of the feathers from the dead galah in his hand.

"Redgum," he asked. "Do you know how to catch a tom cat?"

"I'm sure you'll find a way," the great tree answered.

"Me?" echoed Spindles in surprise. "How could I catch it?"

"Think of a cat as a small lion," said the tree. "And then read what the Bible says about it."

Spindles was more confused than ever. He tried desperately to think of something in the Bible about lions. All he could think of was the story of Daniel in the lions' den. And then he thought of all the lions like small golden pussy cats, with furry manes.

"If lions were as small as cats, they wouldn't be so bad," said Spindles.

"That depends on who you are," said the tree. "To a galah, a tom cat *is* a lion!"

Spindles gulped and nodded his head. Redgum was right.

"Now, here is something for you to read—the rest is up to you. First Peter, chapter 5, verses 8 and 9. Don't forget."

Spindles knew that the conversation was now over. He tried hard to remember the Bible passage. When he rode home at lunchtime, he looked it up straight away. This is what it said:

Be alert, be on watch! For your enemy the devil roams like a roaring lion, looking for someone to devour. Be firm in your faith and resist him.

I suppose a wild cat is like a lion to the birds, Spindles thought. *But how do you "resist" it?*

That afternoon, he talked with Hippie and Tank.

"There has to be a way to catch this cat before he kills any more birds," said Spindles.

"That depends on how clever you're *feline*," said Hippie, emphasizing the last word very carefully.

There was no response.

"Feline . . . Feeling . . . Get it?" said Hippie.

"Me? 'Ow?" said Tank.

"Oh, cut it out, you two," said Spindles. "This is serious."

"Don't get *catty* now," said Hippie.

"And don't *pussy* foot around," said Tank.

"I want some good suggestions, not weak jokes," said Spindles.

"I didn't do it on *purr-puss,"* said Hippie, in a serious fashion.

"Perhaps you should take a *cat-nap,"* said Tank. "That'd solve your problem—if you could nab the cat, then—"

He got no further. Spindles had grabbed a stick and was about to snap it over Tank's back. In a flash, Tank was half-way up a tree and safely out of reach.

"You're absolutely right, Spins," said Hippie. "This is no time for horsing around—er, sorry, for making fun and all that. We really should try to find an answer. But I'm sure I don't know what the answer is."

"I wonder if we could make a trap of some kind," said Spindles.

"A trap?" said Hippie. "What sort of a trap could you catch a cat in?"

"I don't know," said Spindles. "But there must be some way."

"Maybe we could build one?" suggested Tank, still half-way up the tree.

"How could *you* build a trap?" asked Spindles. "You couldn't build anything!"

"I like that!" said Tank.

"Thought you would," said Spindles, smiling for the first time, at outpointing Tank.

"But *you* could," said Hippie. "*You* could build a trap, Spindles. Why don't you give it a go, old chap? Could be rather exciting, actually!"

"Do you think I could?" asked Spindles. "I wonder. . . ."

That night, Spindles spent a long time browsing through the books that lined the shelves in the lounge room. He looked up encyclopedias and other reference books. There didn't seem to be any cat traps anywhere! There were traps like rabbit traps that spring shut on their victims. But he couldn't see a cat getting caught in one of those. There were other traps—like huge mouse traps—that actually killed the animals they caught. But Spindles wouldn't be able to make one—much as he would like to have done so. Then he found what he wanted.

It was a wire cage with a door that would spring shut. With the right kind of bait, you could lure the cat inside and then—slam! you would have him.

With some help from his dad or one of the stockmen, he could make one, he was sure.

Next morning, when Spindles told his dad there was a feral cat on the Range, he asked if he could make a cage. His dad said, "A feral cat, eh? Are you sure?"

"Yes, Dad," answered Spindles. "I'm positive!"

"Well, we don't need cats around here," his dad went on. "See if Butch and Kamulla can help you make a trap."

And it wasn't long before the three of them were all hard at work in the shed—even Spindles helping by holding things and fetching things and doing what he could.

"Well, there y'are, Spins," said Butch, finally. "A trap good enough to catch a lion!"

"It will, too," said Spindles enthusiastically.

"Pretty small lion, son," said Kamulla quietly.

"Not to a bird," said Spindles.

Kamulla chuckled quietly, his bright eyes shining against his black-brown skin. "You're one smart feller, Spins," he said. "One smart little feller."

Spindles grabbed the trap and ran for his pony.

"Where'y goin', Spins?" called Butch.

"To trap the lio—the cat," Spindles called back over his shoulder.

"Haven't you forgotten something?"

"What?" answered Spindles, slowing down just a bit.

"The bait," said Butch. "No tom cat will go in that box without good reason, y'know."

Spindles didn't stop. He just changed direction and headed for the house.

A few minutes later he emerged with a small parcel in one hand and still carrying the trap with the other. He managed to climb on the pony and rode off slowly toward the Range.

"You put the bait here," said Spindles to Tank and Hippie, pointing to a small piece of wire inside the cage."

Tank looked with interest to the spot where Spindles was pointing. Hippie stood with his long neck pointed down and his head close to Spindles'.

"The cat comes in here," Spindles continued, pointing to one end of the cage which was open. "To reach the meat, he has to go right in. The cage is just the right size to contain him."

"Naturally," murmured Hippie.

"Not much good otherwise," said Tank.

"Then when he pulls at the meat, he moves this length of wire and the door slams shut.

Tank and Hippie could see that the door opened inwards and upwards, so that when it fell down you couldn't push it open.

"There's a spring on it, too," said Spindles. "That makes it even more secure."

"Do you think it will work?" asked Hippie.

"I reckon that depends on 'ow 'ungry the old tom cat is," said Tank. "'F'e's 'ungry enough, 'e'll give it a go."

"Well, tally-ho, then," said Hippie. "Splendid idea, actually, when you think about it."

They decided to set a trap at the base of a tree and to put plenty of leaves and stuff around it to try to make it look less suspicious."

"You know what it looks like now?" asked Hippie.

"What?" asked Spindles.

"It looks like someone put a cage under a tree and scattered leaves and stuff around it to make it look less suspicious.

"Well, it's there, anyway," said Spindles.

"You won't fool that tom cat," said Tank. "'E won't go near that unless 'e's really 'ungry. Then 'e'll take the risk. But one thing's for sure. "E'll know that thing didn't grow there!"

Spindles unwrapped the meat his mum had given him and set it carefully in the trap, tying it down so that could not be moved without a struggle. He adjusted the door so that even a slight touch would make it drop down.

The only thing Spindles was really sad

about was that he wouldn't be there to see it.
He would have to leave it overnight.

That night Spindles found it hard to sleep.
He was really excited about the chance of
catching the feral cat. When he finally dropped
off, he slept soundly. But he woke with a start
early the next morning. At first, he couldn't
remember what it was he was looking forward
to. Then suddenly, he knew.

He sprang out of bed and dressed quickly.
He gulped down his breakfast and was soon
galloping out to the Range.

His pony pounded to a stop at the Redgum
tree and Spindles leapt off. He scampered over
to the trap. There was a black patch in the
cage. He must have caught the cat! But to his
great disappointment, it was only a shadow
from the overhanging branches of the
tree—the cage was empty. The bait was
untouched, except for a few busy ants crawling
around it, picking off tiny portions, and
hurrying urgently away to their nest, as if
fearful that the meat would all be gone before
they returned.

But at least there were no more feathers
lying on the ground. So maybe the cat was still
hungry—perhaps hungrier than ever. However,
some of the magpies and parrots had started
to drift back and there was bird-song in the

trees again. If they didn't catch the tom cat soon, there would be more birds killed.

That day seemed to last for a week! All the things that were normally interesting were now boring. But eventually night came and eventually Spindles slept and eventually it was the morning of the next day.

A little discouraged by his disappointment of the day before, Spindles took longer to reach the creek. As he drew near, he realised that something had happened. There were excited bird noises everywhere. He could hear them when he was still a kilometre away. When he reached the creek, he saw a whole group of animals bunched together talking excitedly. Suddenly he realised they were standing around the cage! He urged his pony forward and scattered everyone as he hauled back on the reins at the last moment and stopped almost in the middle of them. There were loud cries of protest, of course, but as the animals drew back, Spindles saw a remarkable thing. There, below him, was the trap. And in the trap was a spitting, snarling, angry black pillow of fur on four legs, poised and crouched, ready to spring at the slightest provocation.

The tom cat's eyes were gleaming and angry. Its mouth was open and its red tongue

and its white teeth seemed all the redder and
all the whiter against its jet-black coat.

Its back was arched and the hairs stood up
like burnt tree trunks in a dense forest after a fire.

"We got 'im!" shouted Spindles.

He jumped down from the horse and bent
to have a closer look. The cat spat at him and
gave a sharp cry. Spindles jumped back in
alarm and trod on Hippie's foot. Hippie pulled
his foot out of the way and kicked Tank in the
face. Tank's head jerked up and collided with
Joey's chin. Joey wandered around dizzily for a
moment or two and headed blindly straight for
the trap. Meanwhile Spindles, unbalanced by
Hippie's sudden movement, had fallen over. He
was struggling to get up, just as Joey walked
forward. The two of them collided and both
fell in a struggling, swirling heap to the ground.

From above them came a loud burst of
laughter. Gleam and some of his friends were
sitting on a branch of a tree. They all rocked
with peals and squeals of amusement.

Joey was rubbing his chin, and Spindles
was brushing dust and dirt from his clothes.
Tank was shaking his head and Hippie was still
hobbling on one leg. They didn't think it was
very funny at all! But it was so good to hear
the birds happy again, that they soon saw the
funny side of things, too.

"Well, you did it, Spins," said Hippie approvingly. "Well done, old chap! Jolly good show!"

"Yeah, good effort, mate," said Tank.

"This is the best news I've had since last Christmas," said Gleam, still perched in the tree. "In fact, it's better. I can't remember when I've been so pleased about something. You've no idea how good it is to see that tom cat in that cage. After the fear and trepidation that we have all been through in the last—"

"Yes, well, quite so, but I think you've made your point, Gleam," said Hippie. "So do be quiet for a while, there's a good fellow."

"But I was only trying to point out that—"

"But what we have to consider now, everyone, is what we are going to do with the cat now we've caught it."

There was an awkward silence. No one seemed to have thought of that, least of all Spindles.

"*Do* with it?" echoed Spindles. "What are we supposed to do with it?"

"Well you can't leave it in the cage forever, old chap, can you?"

"No, I don't suppose I can."

"'Ave you got a bag, Spins?" asked Tank.

"A bag? What for?"

"Well you can always put it in a bag, then drown it or something."

Spindles remembered that there were a couple of old bags hanging over the fence near the cattle grid at the creek crossing.

"There are some bags on the fence. I could get one from there. Then I could put the cat in the bag and take it home. Dad will know what to do with it."

"Wouldn't it be better to let your dad come and get it?" asked Roo quietly. "Then you wouldn't have to do anything."

But Spindles was already picturing himself riding home triumphantly with the cat in the bag. He could see his mum and dad and Butch and Kamulla and Lonely all gathering around, admiring the catch. That would be a lot better than going home empty-handed and then bringing his dad out again. Besides, his dad was busy. . . .

So Spindles ran over to the fence. Five minutes later he was back, puffing and red-faced, with an old bag in his hands.

"Are you sure that one's strong enough?" asked Tank.

"Course it is," said Spindles confidently. "Plenty strong enough."

"Doesn't look in really spiffing condition, you know," suggested Hippie. But Spindles' mind was made up. So he took the bag and fitted it round the entrance of the cage.

"You hold it here, Joey," he said, indicating one corner. "And Tank, you could hold this corner with your teeth. Hippie, could you put your foot down on this part? Then, when I open the door of the cage, the cat will run in, I will close the bag and we'll have 'im."

There was some shuffling and pushing and a few "excuse mes" and "stand backs" and "I've got its." Finally, Spindles said, "Ready?"

They all nodded and so Spindles opened the door. For a few moments nothing happened. The cat still crouched in the cage, its angry eyes glowing like stop lights and its sharp teeth shining beneath curled lips. Suddenly, there was a black blur. Like a cork from a bottle, the cat shot out of the cage, into the bag, quicker than eye could follow. And equally quickly, it burst straight out of the other end! It streaked across the creek bed and up the cliffs on the other side, like a skyrocket gone wild, and disappeared over the top.

Spindles and his friends stood motionless, with the empty bag still in position. They couldn't believe their eyes!

Spindles slowly straightened up. He felt terrible. One moment he was exultant, and excited at his success; the next he was crushed with disappointment, self-blame and shock.

He picked up the bag and folded it over his arms. Then he threw it away in disgust. He turned and kicked the cage angrily.

"Spindles, it wasn't the cage's fault," said Roo quietly.

Spindles burst into tears. "I really wanted to catch that cat," he cried. "And now some more birds will be killed and we'll never catch the stupid thing!"

The other animals didn't know what to say, so they said nothing. One by one they quietly withdrew. Spindles jammed his hands into his pockets and marched toward his pony, which had wandered away in search of grass to a spot near Redgum.

He grabbed the reins and flung himself on to the saddle. He was just about to ride off when he heard his name called. "Spindles!" He stopped immediately. It was Redgum.

"Spindles!" said Redgum. "Don't forget what you read in the Bible."

Spindles said nothing. He turned away and urged the pony homewards.

That night at the meal table, he had an idea. "Dad," he asked. "What other ways are there of catching a feral cat?"

"Why? Didn't your trap work?"

"Well, sort of," said Spindles. And he told his parents what had happened. They laughed at first, but then they did sympathize with him and he felt a bit better.

"Could we get him with a spotlight?" asked Spindles. "Like they do with rabbits and foxes?"

"If we had nothing to do every night except look for one cat, we might," answered his dad. "But the Dusty Range is a big place to look."

"What about the dogs? Could they catch it?"

"Perhaps. But dogs cannot climb trees and cats can—I wouldn't think much of their chances."

"Well, maybe we'll still catch it in the cage."

"Not in the cage, you won't, son," said his dad. "He'll never go in that cage again—not for anything!"

That night, Spindles lay in bed thinking about the tom cat and Gleam and the other birds. They would never be safe while the cat was around. Then he remembered Redgum's words. "Remember what you read in the Bible." What was it, again?

"Be alert! Be on watch! . . . Be firm in your faith and resist him. . . ."

There must still be a way to do it. Perhaps there was some other place in the Bible that would help. He tried to think of other verses, but his eyes were heavy and it was hard to stop his mind wandering, drifting, sliding into the comfortable world of sleep. . . . Suddenly he opened his eyes wide. There *was* another Bible passage. The story of David—of David and Goliath. David had killed Goliath with a stone from a sling. Would that work with a cat? Not a sling perhaps . . . but what about a shanghai? He began to imagine himself lying in a shadowed spot, watching, waiting—just like the Bible said in 1 Peter—alert and ready, his shanghai poised for that old cat to walk right into his aim.

He woke next morning, excited again. This time there would be no mistake.

He decided to make a new shanghai. He searched the creek bed for stones that would be the right size to shoot and to hit a target as small as a cat's head. Then he cut some rubber from a damaged, but new truck tube, strong rubber that would not break, but would transfer all its deadly elastic power to the small missile that would be cradled in the leather grip.

He wanted to wait a week or so until he had practiced enough to be sure that his aim was good. But he couldn't risk the lives of the birds for that long. So he practiced for hours that day, and his aim got better all the time.

He arranged a row of ten tins along a rail of one of the sheep yards. At first, he missed nearly every time. But eventually, he improved. He would hit every second time, and then most of the time. He wished there was someone who could pick up the tins and chase the stones! But he kept on. Then, he lined up all the tins, and one by one, hit all ten of them! Now he was ready.

Butch who had been watching Spindles, and guessed what he was trying to do, wandered to the stockyard. "Here," he said to Spindles, "these will be even better." He opened his hand. There Spindles saw half a dozen shiny, round ball bearings! "You won't miss with these," said Butch.

"Wow! Thanks, Butch," said Spindles, his eyes wide. "I'll get 'im now, for sure!"

Next morning, he explained his plan to his animal friends. The one he had to convince most of all was Gleam. For without Gleam, he couldn't do it. But if Gleam did take part, it would be at the risk of his life!

That afternoon, everything was ready. All of Spindles' friends were out of sight. Tank was hidden on the cliff face across the creek. Hippie was motionless among the mallee—like one of the trees himself, in fact. Roo had taken Joey well up the creek and out of the way. Bilby and Gloria were sleeping—they preferred coming out at night time.

Spindles was lying amongst some bushes,

almost totally hidden from view. Gleam was on the ground, at the foot of a gum tree, picking and pecking at the leaves, and in full view.

Spindles lay there still and quiet. The slingshot near his right hand, ready for instant use. An hour went by. Nothing unusual happened. Two ants were crawling over his legs and he longed to brush them off. A sharp stone was poking into his stomach, and his knee was resting on the point of a stick. There were little black bush flies flitting around his head. They were the most annoying. He felt that if he didn't brush them or slap them or flick them they would drive him crazy. But then he thought of Gleam and the other birds and of the wandering black death that threatened them all. And he lay still.

Another hour went by and still he lay there. The soft breeze crept in under his shirt, caressing his skin like the touch of gentle fingers. *I wish it had fingernails,* said Spindles to himself. *Then it could scratch my back as well!*

Still nothing happened. Perhaps the cat hadn't stopped running yet! Or perhaps he had seen Spindles lie there in the first place and wasn't going to come. But he must be hungry. And if he was . . .

But another half an hour passed and he did not come.

I've had this, said Spindles to himself. *I'll go crazy if I have to stay here any longer. I'm going home. I'll come back and try again tomorrow.*

But just as he began to rise to his feet, he saw something move across the creek. Perhaps Tank was giving up, too. But no, Tank was still on the cliff ledge. Spindles lay still again, watching.

There was another movement, and then Spindles saw clearly what was happening. Creeping low to the ground, its tail flat and its legs bent sharply, was the feral cat. It had its eyes fixed on Gleam. It was still at least fifty metres away, but drawing closer.

Gleam, however, was also somewhat tired of this whole business. At first, he had been very bright and watchful. He knew that if he wasn't, he might not have a second chance. But as time went on, and the sun's warmth spread, Gleam had become increasingly careless.

He would love to have someone to talk to. Even to be quiet for so long was torture for him! And the leaves around him had been picked over so much by now that all he could find was dirt and bits of dusty bark.

He looked in Spindles' direction and called out, "Spins, can we call it a day? This is boring!"

The cat, seeing that Gleam had his back to

it, sprang up and raced toward the bird, its soft paws padding without a sound on the dry earth.

Spindles didn't know what to do. Suddenly everything had gone wrong again. If he called out, the cat would turn away and he would lose another chance to trap it. If he didn't call out, Gleam might be killed!

Gleam took a few steps toward Spindles. Why didn't the boy answer? When Gleam moved, the cat stopped, frozen to the spot like a creek-bed rock, as if it had been there for centuries.

Gleam wondered if Spindles had fallen asleep. "That would be just like him," he muttered. "Leave me out there doing my bit while he dozes his head off. That boy will be the death of me one day!" Gleam did not know how true his words were becoming.

"Spindles!" he called again. "I'm going."

While Gleam spoke, the cat darted forward again. It was now less than ten metres from where Gleam stood.

"Please don't fly away now!" urged Spindles under his breath. "Look around Gleam! Look around!"

Across the creek there was a sudden crashing sound. Gleam looked around in surprise. He couldn't see anything moving.

What had made the noise? Suddenly, there it was again. A large rock rolled off a ledge and fell bouncing and rattling on to the stones in the dry creek bed.

Must be Tank, thought Gleam. *The clumsy blighter.* But then Gleam realised that Tank was not clumsy—not when it came to climbing, anyway. He must have knocked that stone deliberately. Now, why would he do a thing like that?

It was then, with a chill in his heart, that Gleam realised it had been a signal for him! That's why Spindles hadn't answered. The cat must be nearby.

Gleam made out to pick and poke at the leaves again, but his eyes were darting in every direction. And then he saw the cat. It was close! Very close!

Gleam's natural reaction was to shoot into the air, to escape, to fly to freedom. But he forced his feet to stay on the ground. He dug his toes in. He made his head go down to the leaves, his beak to nibble and pick.

He tried to judge whether the tom could reach him in one jump or not. He didn't think it could. Then he tried to see whether Spindles could shoot it from there. He quickly glanced in Spindles' direction. It was too far, and his view seemed to be partly obscured, anyway.

Gleam went on acting as if he had not seen the danger that lay only a few metres from him. He had to lure the cat in closer yet. He hoped he had not underestimated the distance.

He deliberately turned his back on it. He half expected to feel the sudden lunge of its claws in his back and its sharp, angry teeth on his neck. He waited a second or two longer.

Tank squatted like a dead branch on the cliff. He was a long way off, but he could see what was happening. At least that silly bird had turned to face the cat when he had rolled the stones off the cliff. If he hadn't, Gleam might have eaten his last meal that day. Tank watched in breathless excitement as Gleam again turned his back.

Spindles could see what Gleam was doing. He was bringing the cat in closer. Just a few more paces. . . . Spindles slowly raised his shanghai and took careful aim. Now the cat was looking right toward him. He held a careful grip on the small leather pad that held the smooth, silver ballbearing. He pulled it back letting the strong black rubber take up the strain. He wouldn't have two chances—this one had to be accurate. He dared not miss. The cat drew back slightly on its haunches. It was ready to spring, its hind legs already taking the strain for the powerful jump that would bring death to the apparently helpless galah.

Spindles let go of the sling. There was a faint twanging sound and the small, round missile shimmered and flashed through the air like a meteor, past some bushes, past Gleam, past the tree, past a clump of grass—until it landed with a crunching thud right between the cat's eyes.

The tensile, lithe strength drained out of the dark creature's body and it crumpled to the ground, changed in a matter of moments from a powerful, dangerous, lethal machine to a baggy bundle of harmless flesh.

Gleam burst into the air in a flurry of white and grey and pink, and landed, with immense relief, on the branch of the tree, the tension of the last few moments leaving him drained and flat.

Tank jumped up and down with excitement. "You got 'im! You got 'im!" he shouted. "Good on yer, Spins!"

Hippie ran pounding toward them. "I say, what a smashing shot, Spins. Absolutely splendid!"

Spindles climbed stiffly to his feet, kicking his legs to loosen them and get himself mobile again. He poked the shanghai into his pocket, and walked over to the cat. He was a bit afraid that he had just stunned it. But when he looked closely, he saw blood trickling from its nose. It looked very dead.

The other animals were all around him now. They were all talking at once. Somehow, birds were already hearing the news and flying in from all directions, to celebrate.

Later, when Spindles was resting in the shade of the Redgum tree, he asked Redgum, "Was that cat really like the devil, Redgum?"

"Yes, indeed," answered the tree.

"So if I want to overcome the devil, I have to be watchful and alert, too?"

"Yes, just like you were when you were waiting for the cat to attack Gleam."

"I wasn't very watchful when I let it out of the trap, though, was I?"

Redgum didn't answer.

"Redgum," Spindles went on, "I used a shanghai to kill the cat. What should I use to kill the devil?"

"Well, you can't really kill him. But you do have a weapon."

"What is it?"

"I told you that once before."

"When, Redgum?"

"When you nearly got bitten by the black snake."

"Oh, yes, I remember. The Bible—the Word of God. That's my weapon, isn't it?"

"And learning parts of it by heart is like choosing the right missiles for your shanghai. Then you can use them when you need to."

Spindles thought about that. He had been learning a lot about the Bible lately. He certainly needed to know it well.

That night, he told everyone at home how he had killed the cat. And of course he had the body to prove it. They were all very proud of him.

"Perhaps we should have called you David instead of Timothy," said his mum.

"I think I still like Spindles best," said Spindles.

GLOSSARY

Aborigine, an original black Australian.

Alice Springs, the only large town in the centre of Australia.

Aussie, colloquial term for an Australian.

Ayers Rock, the world's largest monolithic rock which stands in the centre of Australia. It is approximately three and a half kilometres long and two kilometres wide.

Bandicoot, a rabbit-sized mammal with a pointed nose. It basically feeds on roots and other vegetation.

Bearded dragon, a rather fierce-looking but actually small and harmless lizard, so called because of a large frill around its neck and its habit of opening its mouth wide in apparent anger.

Beaut, Australian slang for "very good" or "excellent."

Beauty, an expression which means something like "great!" or "terrific!"

Billy, a large can with a lid and handle, something like a paint can in shape and size, used for making tea over an open fire.

Boundary rider, a stockman whose particular task is to patrol the extensive fences of a sheep station. He usually rides either a horse or a motorcycle.

Bush, a wooded area or country land in general, especially in remote areas.

Black boy, another name for grass tree.

Correspondence School, a school for children in remote areas where lessons are conducted both over radio and by mail.

Crow, a black, scavenging bird with a mournful cry.

Darwin, the capital city of the Northern Territory, situated on the northern coast of Australia.

Dingo, a wild dog.

Dinkum, see *Fair dinkum*.

Dog fence, a huge, high fence about eight thousand kilometres long that prevents dingoes from entering sheep country.

Emu, a large non-flying bird something like an ostrich. Usually greyish-brown in color.

Fair dinkum, an expression which means something like "really" or "truly" or "on the level."

Flying Doctor, a medical service in the Outback which provides efficient and speedy assistance to people in remote areas.

Fossick, fossicking, to search or look for something.

Galah, a grey and white cockatoo with pink chest and feathers, and a noisy, high pitched cry.

Goanna, a large monitor lizard which can run fast and climb well.

Grass tree, an unusual bush with a thick stem and a crown of spiked foliage. Usually stunted in growth but can reach a height of five metres or so.

Joey, a young kangaroo, usually still being carried, at least some of the time, in its mother's pouch.

Kangaroo, a marsupial with large rear legs used for leaping, a heavy tail used for balancing and support, smaller forelegs, which are more like arms, and a smallish head. Most kangaroos are about a metre tall, but some reach nearly two metres.

Lino, linoleum.

Lizard, sleepy, a thick, slow-moving lizard about 25 centimetres long with a stumpy tail and a blue tongue. Also called stumpy-tailed or blue-tongued lizard.

Mallee, a scrub-like eucalyptus tree with several trunks, usually growing only to about five metres high.

Mulga, a form of acacia tree, scrubby and untidy. The word "mulga" is also used for a whole area of Outback country, whether there are mulga trees there or not.

Numbat, a termite-eating marsupial about the size of a large rat, which has a bushy tail and a striped back. The official mammal symbol of Western Australia.

Outback, the term used to describe the huge areas of desert and sheep and cattle country in the centre of Australia.

Piton, a spike used by rock climbers to secure their ropes.

Porcupine grass, a prickly grass with long, pointed leaves something like a porcupine"s quills, which usually grows in clumps.

Redback spider, one of the two dangerous Australian spiders whose bite may be fatal. It is small, with a body about the size of a large pea and a red stripe down the back.

Redgum, a large eucalyptus tree which may grow to a height of fifty metres whose wood is a reddish-pink color internally but whose bark is grey or fawn.

Saltbush, a low, grey-green colored bush which grows in dry areas, especially dry saltpans.

Scree, an area of loose stones on the slope of a hill.

Scrub, another name for bush or low wooded country.

Shanghai, a slingshot.

Sleepy lizard, see Lizard, sleepy.

Spinifex, another name for porcupine grass.

Station, a large Australian sheep farm.

Station hand, a man who works on a station.

"Stone the crows," an expression, often of surprise. Similar to "Son of a gun" or "How about that?"

Stockman, a man who works on a station, especially in handling of sheep or cattle.

Sturt Pea, a native Australian plant which grows close to the ground. It has grey-green leaves, something like the leaves on a small melon plant, and distinctive bright red and black flowers. It is the South Australian floral emblem.

Tasmania, the southernmost State of Australia, which is actually an island.

Tasmanian devil, a small dog-like creature with a fierce demeanor and a screeching cry.

Tasmanian tiger, a wolf-like creature with a striped back, which is now probably extinct.

Torch, a flashlight.

Tussock grass, a form of grass which grows in clumps or tussocks.

Ute, short for "utility."

Utility, a small truck. Called a pick-up truck in the United States.

Wallaby, a small kangaroo.

Wedgetail eagle, a large eagle with a tail which has a wedge shape.

Wild hops, a wild flower with bright pink flowers, which was originally imported by Afghan camel drivers as camel feed, but which is now very widespread in some parts of the Outback.

Willy-willy, a small whirlwind or "dust devil."

Wombat, a marsupial that lives in a burrow. It is something like a small bear, fairly slow-moving, and usually quiet and withdrawn.

Yacka, a grass tree.